THE ZALAN BOLT

Celesta Starr

Published by

MELROSE BOOKS 

An Imprint of Melrose Press Limited
St Thomas Place, Ely
Cambridgeshire
CB7 4GG, UK
www.melrosebooks.co.uk

FIRST EDITION

ISBN   978-1-912026-50-0
epub   978-1-912026-51-7
mobi   978-1-912026-52-4

Printed and bound in Great Britain by:
4edge Limited
22 Eldon Way, Eldon Way Industrial Estate
Hockley, Essex
SS5 4AD

He arrived on the night of the Red Lightning bolt, when no sane man, or the most suicidally reckless one, would dare to venture out.

Nobody knew where he came from… Nobody wanted to know.

Do not go out tonight, my friend,
When the skies really rage in revolt.
Do not go out – to never return,
For the dreaded Zalan bolt.

(3rd Seer. Terrian)

Translation from old Yalskrid

Contents

Chapter 1

HELL NIGHT

The first time they saw him, the peaceable inhabitants of the unique old world Sector of the unusual planet Zalan, was that appalling night in the first ira of Spring.

It was the night when the fearful red lightning storm raged the worst for some years, with the deadly circular red bolt giving its awful high-pitched scream every few minutes. These alarming storms, peculiar to Zalan, were the only things that marred the most beautiful and interesting planet in the exclusive Del-Thynne System, although, admittedly, they did keep it from being overrun by 'Utopia' seekers. People visited; yes, thousands of them at all seasons, to see the rare wonders. But they were never tempted to permanently reside with the tempests of renown.

He came out of the bizarre, red-black, howling hell night, like he was a wildly reckless, rejoicing, radiant part of it. Like the shrieking wind, and deluging red-tinged rain, the ground and walls quaking thunder, and the sky scorching, blinding crimson lightning, with its spawned blazing bolt, presented the flaunting, flouting pride of his own strange strength and power, and the darkly shining glory of his aristocratic, but ambiguous, inheritance.

He came as he was to be. That mesmerising, marvellous, malevolent mystery.

Soletra — the lovely, lissom daughter of the proprietor of the Galactic Inn — was to set her wondering, luminous, lime green eyes on him before anybody else. In the general startlement at the authoritative more than imperative banging on the door — surely, nobody should be that insane, or luckless to be out there — the girl of 17 summers went to answer the loud summons on thick grazite wood, being the nearest to it. She opened the door of the charming, old-fashioned tavern as much as she dared for the furies of the elements. Even then, there was more than enough of a roaring, splashing entry, fit to knock her over and drench her.

Soletra flinched, and shivered, and blinked hard to see through the flailing wind, and lashing, sanguineous rain. Her ears winced to the deafening thunder with no sturdy masonry bluntingly in between, if haply it was the re-gathering lull with the lightning child. The brief abatement of its scream that could shatter any sound, and the bravest hearts of men. Soletra, blinking to clear her gaze of the rain, like cold tears on it, was thoroughly prepared for the sorry sight of a scared witless, half dead traveller, who certainly had to be ailing from madness, or misfortune. You were never otherwise abroad, especially in the country regions, on these nights.

The Zalan storms, with their slaying bolts, were no more spoken of carelessly than they were faced, however great the courage or the rashness of the individual. The Zalan populations themselves did, in particular, healthily fear and respect their terrible legacy from that freak of nature eluding remedy and restraint. The locals at the Inn tonight demonstrated this. The current motley selection of faithful patrons had arrived before the storm, which could often strike with no hint of warning, and instant ferocity from serene, calm skies. And every hardy fellow was staying unbudgeably safe in tavern seats, with the soothing Ratzen ale and tobacco, until the wrath was over, able to go as quickly as it had started.

He was a traveller alright, Soletra saw, when she could. But he wasn't half dead! Not by any means. He was absolutely animated, and spectacular in just wetness and dishevel. He had intensely impactive, lively, dartful eyes that were as vividly red as the lightning, and could similarly flash. His heedlessly uncovered hair, curling with the wet, was red and vibrant, falling long about him in riotously rippling reams that could have been living flame. His body, concealed by a profusion of some odd type of cloak as it was, effectively — nigh bristlingly — conveyed its drama of activity, its dynamo of energy, through the blackest fabric swathes tinged with red, like the night, and with a sinister, three-dimensional shine beyond the rain slick.

What! Nobody could look more alive!

And scared witless he wasn't. There was only this glowing exhilaration and elation. Rather, he was the more scaring, in that majestic, magnificent fashion.

He stood haughtily, valley tree taller and straighter, on the flogged, teeming threshold. The rain beat like tiny angry drums on the singular stuff of his cloak, and ran the reflecting red into the black, and vice versa. He threw his regal head airily and exultantly back, with the lengthy, fiery corkscrewings of hair soddenly and stupendously sweeping behind it. Simultaneously, the very lightning seemed to strike from those eyes that had its hot pigment. So intense and electrical was the flash, it could have borrowed from the 30 sizzling prongs branding this night. It fairly sparked along his red curling lashes, and brightly lit up the whole of his face, stamping its every feature grandly and graphically out on the storm hues, and havoc.

Soletra, in her dazed and jolted recoil, had never seen such a face. Zalan men were reputedly as attractive as the women, being nicely rugged and imposing, with their lavish, lustrous, vari-braided hair, and slim, sturdy physique. But they were as plain and dowdy as the Mala bird, compared with this stranger, wherever he was from; it wasn't from here or any near, familiar planet. The face she stared widely at in her frightened thrill and thrall, could have been the work of a master sculptor. It was handsome beyond words and belief, with its flawless symmetry and smooth, youthful, but age-indeterminable skin, like pale, translucent Castel marble.

She drank in the divine details with nervously smitten gulps from a bottomless chalice. The lordly sloping temples. The boldly winging red brows over the devastating eyes, further revealing their exotically slanting shape and sultry, ochre lids. The noble nose curving quick, impetuous nostrils. The chis-elled, extra strong jaw, with the throbful dream of a mouth that was excitingly winning, and warning, in its limitless allure.

But Soletra had never seen anybody like him before. Full stop! She had never envisioned anybody like him. Not in the most unbridled flights of a young girl's fancy. She recoiled again on the wetter spot, with more assembling sensations than she knew what to do about – and a majority of them she didn't know at all. As if things that had slumbered deep, hidden, and totally unsuspected of in the shy, sweet, docile interior of her, had been shaken hard awake in a single, stunning instant.

From his flame rivers of hair to his muddy-booted, active, dominant tread, he seemed next to strike as much as the lightning in his eyes, or the genuine article in the berated, weeping skies. He could have been more than six foot of live voltage, sending little shocks, each of them ablaze, through Soletra, and practically fusing her in her rebound to the floor, where she was becoming more than ever hazardously exposed to the Celestial tempest.

The stranger smiled sardonically at Soletra's overt reaction to him. But there was a more stirringly sensual side to the smile, and his fire eyes, with the spark-skimming lashes, had their interest on the whetting stone of that sensuality for the lovely, tremulous, transfixed obstacle in his path. Then, in his continuing blatant disregard for bigger hazards from the wicked weather, he performed the graceful bow that owed more to mockery and scorn than actual courtesy, and spoke over another ominously building thunder roll, through crimson flash, and wind, and rain pound,

'Well, my pretty. As a long, lone traverser on foot, may I not step into your humble, but presently welcome abode? Or must we both be hacked to pieces by the gale, drowned by the downpour, or hit by the re-birthing bolt?'

His voice suited his formidably fascinating, fervid attraction, that rippled a hundred more known, and unknown, thrills strung on jolts through the bemazed Soletra. Never had she heard such a voice. Efficiently versed in the Zalan language, discounting a lilt of an intriguing accent, it was a many coloured voice. It was melodiously clear as vedellan crystal, immersed in the flame of his eyes, but catching on colder blades, low in shades spelling 'beware'; yet silk soft, and pulsant, and rich, and mellow as the Worship bell, with its same way of carrying far in stillness and storm. As it was carrying now. Over the storm. With a collecting ring to it, like an iron hammer on the preserved old Zalan anvil. Calling one to worship him.

'Do forgive me, Sir!' A rush of flurry and flounder propelled Soletra from her freeze of fear-flavoured rapture. She moved in malfunctioning Droid jerks to admit the overwhelming personage, and was vigorously blinking again, in her greater dazzlement and daze, not the driving rain any more.

He surveyed her from the torrent for a burning second or two longer. All of her, as she reversed into the drier precincts of the Inn. As if he cared for it the more, the minutes' work of storm on her. Her splashed and blown, riper lime green hair escaping abundantly from its severe bun for kitchen toil. Her lime green eyes, and the more flushed, cream petal complexion of her angelic face, with the raindrops glistening on them like tears or jewel fragments. Her slender, but curvaceous figure, twice as obvious in the already wet dress and apron starting to cling to it.

The always modest girl felt an unusual spurtlet of gratification amidst the bewildering everything. And she didn't remedy a slack hairpin, or wipe off a globule of water.

After that. In he came.

In he came. To that cacophonous clap of thunder renewing its seismic effects on ground, walls, and foundations. The screechiest gust of wind whisking the deluge wilder. The painfully brightest lightning flash painting the night just a blistering, blood red. And that latest frizzled-out dread bolt back forming above the thrashed Xylax trees, too close on those borders of the pond-logged yard.

In he came. With all his dark-veined drama and majesty, and all his aura-ised mystical powers and might. An entrance which could have rivalled for import that of the bolt itself the door was blessedly shutting to, and which could have shaken impossibly more of the 'Moon Star' Tavern and everybody in it, who were never to forget the night that was really to have no end…

Chapter 2

ZALTAR VALADA

The Tavern, handed down through two generations of Soletra's family, was a superior example of that Sector's ingeniously manufactured old world culture. Constructed of the local mottled grey stone, with local slate roof, and squat, slate chimney having its discreet rod, it was a deliberately lopsided place, boasting embedded, latticed windows, and arching, hunching, huge knobbed doors. All the right trimmings to authentically steep it in the character and charm of Zalan's picturesque past. It was also as friendly and comfortable a place as you could wish to find planet-wide.

The main room inside — for the drinking, smoking, and prudent gaming — was large and low ceilinged, and looked even more lopsided. It had traditional bare stone walls, and a wealth of sepia rafters decked with glinting copper moons, and stars, or copper stellate lamps with lasting tallows of multicoloured flame. Crescent moon tables of polished mirror wood, and matching chairs cushioned in orange, were situated cosily around the room, in pleasant range of the cheery log fire. The enormous, carved stone hearth, with bow-legged fire dogs, nearly claimed one wall.

The bar down the opposite bulging side was another glinting

medley of octangular and triangular bottles, and tall, fluted, frosted glasses mingling with burlier copper tankards. And on the spick and span counter were true antique, copper-headed pumps, a hulky cash dispenser, and a casual strewing of old-fashioned, emulating bar towels, advertising the meritorious ale. The rest of the room was made up of the novel window side, and the various crouching inner doors leading to the surprisingly expansive regions beyond, and the just as characterful quarters for Soletra and her parents, and the staying guests.

That night there was a big fire in the grate, with the wind whistling down the chimney making the flames erratically dance. And the thick orange curtains at the windows were all tightly drawn over the fortified panes to at least keep the storm view at bay.

The fabulous, forbidding stranger swept to the centre of the room, leaving the wet Soletra obscured in his darkly brilliant shade. The girl, who was starting to feel like a creature of the hated storm herself, was content in shivers to be eclipsed, and watch the man more avidly.

He halted lithely and livelily on the fringes of one of the woven scatter rugs that warmed slabstone, and below a swinging, squeaking lamp at which the intrusive wind had moaningly snatched. The lamplight blown colourless varnished his settling fires of hair, now to go with the hearth fires too, and his blackly settling, exorbitant cloak that concealed his whole body. In the settlings that seemed to have the hiss of the rain in them, and the hint of whispers, more than the swish, the red of his hair then vehemently clashed with the no longer lightning-tinted blackness of the cloak. The red of his hair. And of his eyes. That brought the lightning hue, and a bit more of the pronged peril, inside.

Water dripped from his steadied eddies of cloak into pools at his feet. An exaggerated pit-patter on mat, and stone. He just stood there in the drippings. Just redoubtably reared there, with a new warning throb of his might that was as much as his magnificence, and a discernable threading of the sly and sinuous through his grace. He silently and scornfully observed his surroundings in their convincing designs of the past, his uncanny red gaze narrowing to cunning slits, like a Lectan cat's, arriving to linger on the Taverner and his wife, and their eleven patrons. All these worthy folk who, after their first amazement at somebody rapping on the door in a Zalan storm, had secondly been considerably offset by the dumbfounding appearance of that somebody visibly thriving on the crazed elements.

The hardy handful of fire-hugging regulars awaiting the calm, with their appeasing ale, pipes, and a good tale or few, stared back at the stranger over the profound pause in whatever they were doing. The interesting blend of male faces — young and personable, middle aged and distinguished, old and vari-wrinkled — all holding their startlement, to lowered tankards, and smoke-furling pipes.

Soletra's portly, brindled-haired landlord father, Rhada, who'd stopped in mid-sort of more scented logs for the fire, stared as roundly as his loyal customers. He was as startled as anybody by this man, in spite of being well accustomed in his trade to all kinds of things and persons. He'd especially had rife acquaintance with visitors from other Worlds, with their claim to the extraordinary, or the bizarre, the grotesque, or the weird, the unreal, or the hideously malformed. Like it was with his comely, plump wife. Illana, with her viridescent locks neatly plaited, had just emerged from the kitchen, and was frankly gaping, and close to dropping her tray of Sater cakes steaming from the oven.

The sensational traveller mockingly bowed again to every one of them. The cloak sounded to be whispering about him, though he scarcely moved it. Whisperings devious and clandestine… Scheming, and conspiring…

And every one of them went on staring at him. Persistently, without a word. Which wasn't typical behaviour by any means. Zalan people were always warm-hearted and exceedingly hospitable, whether they were pleasuring, or not, but had their troubles. They were that benignant a race, these sowers of peace not war, and the resultant reapers of love and prosperity. This said it in volumes for the category the mysterious stranger was in.

The Taverner, Rhada, rallied before anybody, lurching his prided role of the genial host through his inhabitual qualm for another. 'Forgive our surprise that makes us unforthcoming, Sir,' he said, in his not as resonant tone, and with the smile of his vocation forced. 'But you are completely unexpected, and that is putting it mildly. Nobody is ever out in our storms, if they can help it! Homes are immediately sought by residents, should they strike suddenly, and our conveniently located emergency shelters by any caught travellers. And if I may remark, from the duration of this storm, you in the latter plight should have sought refuge quite a while ago. Are you that astonishingly uninformed about the Zalan bolt—?'

The stranger, deigning to speak himself, cut more

ungraciously in on him. The response in the silk-encased, heated iron and knife, reverberating queerly round the snug room. If that room was still as snug. With the fellow surely bringing in the dank chill of the night, and discordant strains of the storm, and the something indefinably dark about him alongside the gloss.

'That screaming scarlet circle of fire out there. It poses no problem to me!' he declared. 'More it fascinates and excites me!' An unheard-of response! Nudging at ridicule! It certainly signified rashness at its peak! It was, in a concept, sacrilegious. Startlement was piled on top of startlement.

'But, forgive me again, Sir. You cannot possibly know the horror of the bolt!' Rhada had to say aghast, on falters no more his wont. 'The deadly danger for unprotected man, or beast, buildings, or environment!'

'And tell me. How are you all protected?' the stranger asked, with a sneering humour.

'The houses, and the people inside them, by the conductor rods on the chimneys,' Rhada replied, faltering on. 'And the environment and the wildlife, by similar, more camouflaged rods that are activated and raised on signals from our sophisticated hillside warning systems. Systems, unfortunately not infallible, with some of the storms apt to hit with no pre-threat, but their instant fury all at once. As you will have seen today.'

'Not that sophisticated an Alert Post!' the fearfully incredible man leered, adding after poignantly poised seconds, 'But I do know of the bolt. Better than you may think!' He seemed to strike again, like that lightning and its spawn he dared to disparage, in the room and upon them all.

Everybody who could have fancied that the insulated

interior of the Inn turned a sizzling blood red for a rent moment, that they felt red shards piercing them to the awed, rocked bone, and even smelled the sulphuric vapours. Such was the progressing play of him on the minds that were unluckily more susceptible to him because of the Zalan sway to superstition. A bent particularly prevalent in these areas dedicated to the inspirational past.

What Rhada, his wife, and patrons didn't fancy when the moment was by, and, not, was the prickling, shiverful unease creeping up on their startlement, and the room that was 'creep-ing' too, into more of the cold, for all the warm hearth, and decidedly into shadow.

Only Soletra had lesser misgivings for more spellcast, heady wonder, her prickles the pringles of thrill. And for what other curious, baffling, unrecognisable, and ungraspable affairs had been roused in those unplumbed depths of her.

The stranger merely smiled at them all. A supercilious smile that never touched his banefully superb eyes. Instead, the eyes more hotly impaled the fireside party and hosts – not Soletra – in his blindingly bright wake, where they caused to be evident another disconcerting trait of them. They were utterly unreadable and unfathomable behind their malign, mocking, unnerving red lightning sheens, but they themselves could probe acutely and capably into other eyes… and fiendishly farther… As if they could open the however well barred doors of the mind, and the heart, and the very soul, and look right in… Giving one to believe, on a new uncomfortable route, that no thought or emotion was sacred. No secret safe.

There was a longer pause, that let the hush of the louder sound of suspense into it. That clawed with iced nails into shrinking nerve edges, and more grossly magnified the storm din, with the crowning scream of the still terribly near bolt.

And then the careering hearth flames flung the real shadow of him, they somehow took from behind him, on Rhada, Illana, and the villagers. As if it had become separate from him – on Soletra it had been that shadow of dazzle. On the others, it was darker than the room shadow he had wrought, and felt more wetly cold on tense flesh, as rain water would. And despite the munificent cloak sketched it shapeless, there was that ill impression of still some awful shape.

The rigidly dormant breath-stuck-in-throat recipients upgraded the shiver they all shared.

When he did speak once more, to Rhada, they all shared a start. 'But, Taverner, I would like a warm by your fire, and a receptacle of your fine-looking ale,' he said, with the continuing much else underlying the words, and the voice.

Rhada re-rallied on the jarrings of his start. 'Of course! Of course! I am being inexcusably remiss. Come. Come closer to the fire, and I will see you have a tankard brimming with undeniably the best ale in the land,' he bade hastily, prone to fuss out of all character. 'And do try a local cake which my wife, Illana, has just baked.'

Illana, a fluttering fly in swatter shade, struggled with a slipping tray.

'I require the ale alone.' The stranger headed for the hearth in his unnatural whisperings of cloak, the regulars rallying, too, at his emphatic approach, but only doubling their discomfort, doubt, and suspicion, as they sat more erect in their chairs. They watched warily when he halted where he wanted to be, which was unwantedly nearer to them, with his hands sleeking from the concealment of his cloak to undo it by the black ties, and remove it. Everybody glanced at his hands. They were pale and slender, with long, tapering fingers, a left index finger partially obliterated by a red-gemmed ring, and they were as disquieting in their swift, sly grace and express aliveness, as he was. The ring flashing to his adroit hand movements, could have had a sliver of the red lightning in that.

He slid the swirlsome cloak from him, and before Rhada could relieve him of it, dropped it to his feet as another pool in blackest black. Rhada could have been slower for staring with everybody — and nobody more than Soletra — at the revealed figure of the daunting enigma. He was just as spectacular here. It was further perfection and wholesale man, girded in utmost elegance. A tight-fitting, laced-up, shiny black shirt sensually stressed his smoothly muscled, long, lean arms and virile chest, with gaps in the lacings permitting inviting glimpses of the red hair on that chest. A broad, big-buckled belt enhanced his narrow waist. And trousers, black and shiny as his shirt, glided splendidly over his lean, curving, firm, pulsative hips and thighs, and on down over his long, lean, athletic legs into the shin-hugging boots.

Yet, as Soletra's already disarrayed senses were dashed to the wall and into bits and pieces by the outstanding bodily attraction to complete him, Rhada and company saw with their warier eyes what wasn't as attractive. They saw all that the shapeless shadow could have implied. That figure in its super slick and erotic garb was the epitome of the slyness and guile previously made just perceptible. It was downright reptilious. In the semblance of the Hedlar snake. The beauteous, but vicious and deadly venomous King of the Zalan junglelands.

You could quite detect it in the figure. The hypnotically gracile, lovely, and horrible waving of the Hedlar death dance.

This unneeded more which fed the unease and discomfiture, as Rhada had fed the fire.

Smiling sardonically at the ill influences he'd bestowed and increased, the stranger leaned in his slyer, slideful suppleness to warm himself over the fire. If he could have warmed it – with his eyes! He didn't have to dry his slinky apparel, there being no speck of damp in it. The cloak must have been more than amply weatherproof. It was only his red mane of hair that was wetly glistening. And the clear, unblemished skin of his sculpted face with the dissolving rain drops on.

Rhada belatedly, and charily, attended to the well serving cloak. With the never unhappier host nearly letting it out of his chubby hands again, when it was exactly like picking up folds of nauseous slime. Whatever the fabric was — which he couldn't identify— it wasn't agreeable on getting wet.

'I'll put this to dry, Sir,' Rhada said, attempting to mask his distaste and maintain his loathing grip on the cloak. His tenser voice the louder for it, had its own peculiar, unpertaining echo in the quiet and unquiet room. Not encouraging him any the more.

'Illana,' he said to his worriedly watching wife, 'pull the gentleman's ale for me.' The Taverner knew she would prefer to do that, in lieu of coping with the revolting cloak. The woman nodded, jitteringly depositing the ignored tray on an available table, and doing it with a resounding clatter on wood and higher keyed nerves.

'I would be grateful.' He said it sarcastically, the traveller in midnight black, but with the flaring red eyes, and hair, and ring on his finger. He inclined closer to the old-fashioned grate, his hauntingly handsome and disturbing features extra distinct in the fuller ruddy glow, his raiment shimmering about him more sensually with that added slyness. It was his gaze that didn't reflect the log lights. Having those fires in it enough.

Some of the anxious gathering could have thought that the hearth flames pranced more berserkly to him and his, than they did to the dirgeful wind in the chimney mouth. They had a more hollow whooshing to them, drowning the cracking and spitting, and had never been as much like tongues, greedily lapping up the live sparks galore.

'Will you also be wanting a bed for the night? We are empty until the tourist shuttle,' Rhada inquired politely more than enthusiastically, and brooking no delay in transferring the cloak to the 'olde hook stand' left of the fireplace. To the scurry in his hurried step came the creak of a chair from an all at once restive patron, and the clack of another setting down his abandoned pipe in fingers changed to thumbs. The first sounds of motion from the staring, stupefied sitters, the first actual sounds from them, that were magnified themselves.

'No,' was all the stranger said, as Illana clumsily pumped ale and flooded a tankard.

Rhada embraced relief for that. And for leaving the detestable cloak in its slippery shimmers, with water pittering onto the mottled stone floor, shadowy drippings that could have been diluted slime… The taverner went to rescue Illana, fretfully demoted to amateurish messings at the bar. As he mopped at the bubbly brown spills, the thunder burst into one of its most deafening peals of the night, a crescendo to split 'Celestia's symbols', along with eardrums under sufficient duress. And the bolt sonorously screamed its loudest, still topping the thunder, indicating it was only nearer to the Inn. Neither was the wind lagging, with its fury launching it into critical force and its version of a boom to its roar, and howl. It drove through the teeming rain, with a violence to veritably part the sheets of water down the middle, like a parting sea, and it smashed against the building to belabour it blacker and bluer, and shake and rattle the fortunately unbreakable windows more than ever, in the way of something determined to get in. Or enable the unholy bolt to.

Soletra — bedraggled and half sodden — unnoticed yet by her parents and everybody, wasn't at all hearing the storm any longer. She was that engrossed in being bewitched closer to the darkly wondrous visitor. Bewitched in the true fateful style of the hapless beholder of the Hedlar. Closer and closer she moved in the sapping clutch of unfought mesmerism. Her eyes glassing, her flushed cheeks a throb, her lips revealing soft, constricted rags of breath.

Closer. And closer.

A customer, oblivious of the girl levelling with him, spoke at last, in the thunder's down roll. His taut, brittle timbre terminating the uncommon silence of him and his friends. It was a young man, with braided beige hair, and the beige stubble of a prospective beard on his chin. Prior to that imperious banging on the door, he had been telling the merriest tall tales to his placid peers.

'Are you just passing through, Sir? An early walking tourist?' he asked, courteously and hopefully. And with his own abnormal echo. It wasn't like speaking in this always rosily cheerful room any more, but as if they had all been spirited off to a subterranean cave, or a tomb of their ancestors.

The answer to the question wasn't given straightaway. The stranger stared intently into the hearth burning in conjunction with him. But, when the question wasn't repeated by the young man and his fading bravado, or by anybody having none, the troubling traveller suddenly unbent and swung swiftly and insidiously round, his hair flaming onto his black shoulders. Everybody jumped afresh in their chillier skins, and hearts missed more than hitting.

Soletra herself started to a stop the attained inches from him, knocked out of her trance and nervily half tumbling over her vacillating feet.

He resumed all his imposing height on his turn, and his eyes darkly and redly had worse yet for the paler ring of faces. It wasn't only the burningly plainer threat and malice, but that something else smouldering lower behind it. That something else with no name, and no description, that now brought proper fear. Fear that was new… And fear that was old… Making scalps and spines bristle, blood congeal, and flesh virtually crawl.

Tankards positively shook in abstractly preserved grasps, slopping froth over the sides. The fidgets that had begun were checked by a rooting to chairs. Somebody dropped, not put, a battered pipe onto the table, with a thrice magnified noise in the worsening quality of quiet that elongated the latest jumps more out of the skin than in.

He feasted more sumptuously on his cowing of those not generally cowed, and said in that deadlier fascinating voice seeming to more than before flash forth its bell-toned syllables to conform with his eyes, 'Permit me to announce. I am Zaltar

Valada. Wanderer of the stars. But where I come from, where I have been, and where I yet may go, is my business alone.'

And him saying it, more luridly aglow in the hues and echoes of the storm he could have belonged to, and it to him – with something else here, too, that could have been standing next to him…. that had no form, and no countenance, and no place in the realms of men.

Chapter 3

THE UNSPOKEN

He drank Rhada's prided ale with enjoyment, but no comment. He drank to the dregs, but haughtily refused a refill. He slid his empty tankard nobody was disposed to take, onto the 'aged' mantelshelf, and with a slender, artful hand resting on the shelf looked back into that wilder fire. His face was stroked anew by the rapid, related red flickerings, with his eyes revelling on in their mockery, malignance, potency, and portent, and the bloodstone ring sparkfully joining in.

Only minutes had gone by, stretched to tormenting hours as they had been on the rack of fraying nerves. However after that last climaxing storm force, the frightful weather was showing the extra prayed-for signs of wholly going the other way. Of subsiding. Like it could. The subsiding that could be as quick as the eruption. A one solitary boon about it all.

The Moon Star patrons couldn't be thankful enough for their impending excuse to leave, though they still hunched together, watching in now eerie awe the self-professed Cosmic roamer, whose very name was somehow not to be said, or even housed in thought. 'Stranger' was adequate for the strange, and the fearsome, and – the imagined, while unimaginable more… The tavern's hosts, not to be as imminently released from shadow as the traveller showed no signs of going, kept uneasily industrious. Rhada was making a weighty pretence of re-adjusting his pumps. And Illana was tremblingly wiping tables, and plumping unused seat cushions in that dark, vital vicinity.

Soletra, that sole exception under enchantment more than superstitious fears, had just been banished to the kitchen and undone chores. Her parents, abruptly reminded of her presence by a gloatingly interested red gaze pointedly back on her, had been that desperate to get her away from him that her blown and wet condition hadn't registered on them at all. The girl, inwardly remonstrating with extremely untypical fervour, was untypically snubbing unwashed crockery stacked in the sink to sneakily stare on at him, via the fraction of space she'd left between door and jamb.

She had been utterly unable to relinquish that unprecedented vision of him, with – or not – the forbidding and the foreboding side of his Sorcerer's spell. She was indeed his Hedlar-ified hopelessly and helplessly enraptured captive, right to that ambiguously instigated deep of her, where he made a dark, delectable thrill out of her every brand-new emotion from there. Including the misgivings. She simply couldn't recover from that face which broke the mould for dark wonder. That was irresistible, dangerously exciting and enticing, with its supreme looks in the fulgence of the presiding eyes, and its flamboyant, flame frame of hair drying thicker and curlier, and spraying a tantalising lock over the arcing brows and heavy eyelids. And she could recover less from that supreme figure, so long and lean, with its streamlined muscles of the leashed lethal power, but its wily snake grace, the aliveness and zest electrifying that, and the paraded, pulsing manliness to the core.

The face and figure that wove the fabric of dreams. If Soletra had never aspired to these dizzying summits. Mere mortal minds could never conjure the equal. Awake. Or sleeping.

The face and figure of a dubious Deity in descendance.

He stayed in this jeeringly, warningly aloof and grandiose attitude, and in his explicit silence since his main deterring words with the unspoken, until the storm was dying outside beaten, bruised walls. Until the scream of the bolt had sheared off entirely, to be buried in the grave of the lowering thunder and instantly ceasing wind, and rain, and the hangdog group of Rhada's patrons were punctually grabbing at the coveted cue for indisputable flight.

Many chairs scraped in loud unison, with deserted tankards clunked askewly down, for deserted smoked-out pipes to be scratted up, and stuffed – ash and all – into tunic pockets. Four of the men rose cumbersomely at once, and others hurriedly followed suit in an erratic clump, every cringeful eye eschewing the stranger who had ruined their night more than the storm, then going sheepishly to Rhada. The villagers felt they were forsaking their good host and friend. But they couldn't help it. Not on this occasion. A variety of mumbled goodnights were stunted on the air now so oppressive it could have been black-leaded; the men wincingly bending their heads, and trooping to the door in ones and twos, endeavouring not to be seen to be rushing.

'Have a care,' Rhada bid them, dejectedly watching them go. But understanding.

'And you, Rhada. Illana.' A couple of the men mumbled

that, too. With no backward glance.

The no-happier Illana nodded to them as she wiped that same table for the fifth fumbling time. It could have been a sixth when the customers passed, with the odd scudding step, into the incredibly calmer, reinstated sloe black night, and vanished into it. The dribbles of rain from flogged eaves and leaves, their fading squelchier treads, swallowed by the dour remnants. When they might never have been.

Only Soletra didn't mind the loss of the locals. In her spell-struck blindness.

The stranger then magnificently mobilised. All jabbing red glisters of hair, and gaze, and contrasting black, softly sensual, and seductive shimmers of vestment.

He spoke sneeringly to the baulking Rhada and his wife, with their peeking, dissident daughter pricking her ears back up in her semi-swoon.

'Talkative fellows, hey, Taverner?'

'Pardon them, Sir.' Rhada vocally scrambled into more undue apology. 'They aren't usually so reticent, and they certainly didn't mean to be uncivil, or disrespectful. They were just – surprised. Surprised by you coming out of the awful storm as if it was nothing. By – er – you altogether, Sir.'

'May I construe that as a compliment?' He sneered.

'You may! You may!' Rhada gushed.

'You may!' Illana managed to loosen her tightly tied tongue to hastily and stutteringly agree.

'Oh. You can speak, woman.' The red eyes smirkingly scalded her into farther retreat.

'Are you really averse to a bite of supper, Sir? Before you go yourself?' Rhada swiftly intervened.

'Before I go myself.' The stranger took him up on that with an underlined hot silk jibe.

'Let me rephrase it. Should you have to leave. As I've said, you are welcome to a room for the night,' Rhada sped to rectify, if it was his last desire of the decade to do it.

'No. I shall be going momentarily.' At his taunting slow pace, the man with the name not to be said, again relieved the landlord and the cloth-kneading Illana, to their floor-chaffing shoes. Soletra was still the exception, with her acutest disappointment. It would have been another dream to have had somebody like him spending the night beneath their modest roof. 'I trust my cloak will be dry.'

'It will. Being on that hook nearest the hearth.' Rhada pledged it the more stoutly for his reliance upon that. 'And my wife can pack you victuals for your journey I hope will continue well.'

'I'll wager you do, Taverner!' The stranger gave a short, scornful laugh, but his eyes were fiercer daggers of fire. 'Only it is a no to the victuals. I have all that I need with me.' This reminded Rhada, in his battled tendency to shield his stabbed eyes, that the dismaying man wasn't carrying a thing. Not a strap, or a stitch of a traveller's satchel. And had the Innkeeper puzzling over it in between his quailings.

Whatever. He hadn't lied, Rhada's persecutor. In that said matter of moments, he was whirlsomely donning his just as 'slimy' cloak – whether dry or not – and, with his hair flaming onto the vile, slippery, and weirdly whispering blackness, was preparing to depart into the tamer night.

'Thank you for your hospitality of a sort,' he said derisively to Rhada, when he'd refastened his cloak and was re-engulfed

in the sickly oily, obsidian slidings, and the secretive whisperings as invidious as him. To Illana he ridiculingly inclined his
strange and resplendent head, having her jumpily fit to curtsy,
as if to a Laadran Royal condescending to thus acknowledge
his lowliest subject.

. And before he fluidly swung in slides and whispers
towards the door, he glanced right across in the direction of the
hiddenly peeping Soletra, with her heartfelt sigh that did have
his name in falters of thought in it, and spoke with his leer and
disdain dipped into the sensual.

'Goodnight to you also, my pretty. And who knows? Our
paths could meet again. They very much could.'

Soletra sprung back in her sweet shock. Nearly as far as the
knotted wood cooling cabinet. But her spurt of rash, impulsive
joy was sweeter for what was to her the unmistakable promise
in his voice. A promise – just from him to her…

Rhada and Illana could yet be jolted by him there. But they
didn't guess about Soletra's infatuated and unknowingly canny
green eye that had been in the crack of a gap. And any promise
was mislaid for them in their fear and unrest. They surmised
he'd only called to their doted-on daughter in his smugly
smiling insolence, and temerity of the highest order.

The stranger walked to the door in his contemptuously
smiling arrogance, his almost crackling aliveness, his surrepti-
tious, serpent smoothness, and with whatever else that could
be there with him – that the cloak hellishly slid, and whispered
to also. But he had to have a final recondite remark in a starker
mode for Rhada and Illana, who inordinately couldn't wait for
that door to shut and lock on him.

Slightly pausing against the re-opened night, looming

more broodingly black and preyfully blood-eyed, he said, 'You cannot stop wondering about the likes of me, inquisitive Taverner and his wife. And you could only learn to wonder it more. But hear me in this that never comes truer.

'We are not all what we seem. And. We do not all seem what we are…'

Chapter 4

'WHAT IS HE – MORE THAN WHO?'

The next day, when everything should have been washed amendingly brighter after the storm, the skies were tawny, stone-heavy, and still weepy. A ghostly mist enveloped the area, hiding what damage there could be from that particular night of nature's ferocity.

The slowly whirling density with the same tawny tints made lost horizons of the distant, tattered, cloud-grazing mountain tops, and the gigantic green and turquoise falls foaming wearingly down their sheer sides. It created irksome contours and configurations from the lower saffron hills, and slopes kicked miles by the mountains' gashed feet, and from the craggily-banked, ultramarine mirror lakes, and pink and yellow patchwork meadows. It tornly draped the nearer lush, rainbow forests, where burrowing flowers damply overslept, and the streams on loan from the lakes in their crystalline slitherings. It stealthily wound through the adjacent blue valley, which all the above beauty backclothed, and the so authentic, picturesque old world village of Kratana that nestled obliquely in the valley depths by its own quicksilver stream.

'It's like a day of mourning,' said Soletra's mother. The

woman was subdued and jittery yet from last night, as she stood in the unaiding gloom of the spick and span kitchen. She spoke as she rubbed her hands on her snow-white apron, and looked out of the embedded latticed window at the immediate phantom vicinity that was the Inn's spacious, genuinely cobbled yard. They were all abstruse formations groping their way in the rainy mist. The Xylax trees edging the orange vine climbing wall around the yard. The sprawl of outbuildings as artistic and museum-ified as the house, with the thicker vine cowl. And the show-stopper, antiquated, square stone well that could draw sparkling water from the original effervescent spring.

The Moon Star Tavern was located quaintly and impressively on the crest of the valley, and advantageously close to both the main Travellers Shuttle road, and the branching-off rougher path delightfully descending amidst floral bushes and purple copses to the village. It was that blossomy mite closer to the path and the view of this to the tree-screened village, which was the loveliest and most effectively ancient hamlet in the Sector, deserving its title of being the chief tourist attraction there. It was a pity the place was screened. It would have been another big bonus for the Inn to have had priceless glimpses of Kratana in the Vale. All those fairytale cottages huddled crookedly on crooked, narrow, cobbled streets; the crooked, bulgier shops in the crooked, flower-adorned space in the middle; and the traditional mill and wheel that turned with its realistic aged creaks, and the melodious song of water. Rhada could just sell the Guide Brochures, and books on local folklore and legends that had become based in the village, and were as charming, winsome, and inveigling as it was.

'Our creepy star wanderer must have upset the normal weather more than the storm did!' the Taverner chuntered, sitting listlessly with his pipe as burled as Xylax bark he was putting before his hearty breakfast that morning. In the light of day, dingy as it was, he was feeling guilty and ashamed about his actions last night. He, who was no coward, had unarguably been one then. Why, he'd marginally grovelled in front of the brilliant, baleful stranger!

But, on the other hand, he was no braver in regard to the fellow today. He remained as jittery as Illana. Especially having had a string of bad dreams about him, and awakening in the dreary dimness of that dawn to know only the nourishing of the uncomfortable, unmanning, unreasoning fears.

'He is a dark being, that,' he added, in a manner to console himself. 'And I vow we shall feel the shades of him for a while, even if with luck we don't see his face again.'

'May we never do that!' Illana had to shiver, moving unsettledly from the window. She hadn't had the nicest dreams of him either, albeit her wakings had been more in relief. 'I won't rest, I'm sure, until he has clear gone from here, and better, back to where he came from. Wherever that can possibly be.'

'And where, is the question that might be best to stay as a question.' Rhada muttered, unsteadily inhaling.

Soletra, seated by herself at the table under the rafters, listened to her beloved parents in their loitering disconcert. But she didn't say a word over her differently unwanted plate of grilled rolan eggs and spinner beans. And over her fast, fervent heart thumps enough to vibrate the patterned wood table her elbows were digging into, and the straddle legged chair she was perched on.

She had dreamed of the stranger, too. But only excitingly and incitingly. In the deceptive spangles of her marvel and entrancement. Seeing him with the lightning on his gorgeous tumult of hair, in his magical, mystifying eyes, and glancing off the theatrical sweeps of his shiniest cloak about that super sexy figure and attire. And she had only woken with the depressing dawn to protest they had just been dreams.

She had then, in fact, laid there in such a bewildering, throeful force of longings and desires her gentle, innocent disposition should never have been capable of, for that meeting up with him once more. As he had promised.

As he had promised – hadn't he? To her ears alone. And she had actually been so distracted by all this and her seemingly commencing change overnight, that Edrak, her childhood sweetheart and betrothed, with whom she'd always had a blissfully happy, contented relationship – could have no longer existed to her.

And never could have.

As the morning progressed, the mist began to go. Stealing in its tarnished gauze dribs and drabs back to the mountains' shaggy top knots, where it hung in slowly lightening shreds to a vague sun behind it. Eventually the laggard sun burst brightly free, completely dispersing all fradgy fog leftovers, and taking up its belated recompense after the storm.

The spirits of Rhada and Illana struggled to rise with the sun. The benevolent pair, hoping its blessed golden radiance would push that ghastly night farther aside, into the category of a bad dream itself. But struggled was the operative word. It wasn't as easy as they would have supposed. That night filtered inexorably on into the improving day, keeping – as Rhada had woefully predicted – the shadow of it and its stranger, to have it slink furtively along walls and beams like some tangible thing. All man and wife could do, by mutual consent, was shake the dogged dark and its provider out of any of their conversation, as a Shala hound does icy water from its fur, and apply their concentration to the disclosed storm damage for them.

Surprisingly, the gale's vandalism was minimum for that roaring excess. The unbowing Xylax trees – these sturdiest of trees, having roots to the bowels of the earth – had amputated limbs, and ripped off foliage, and vines were half peeled from their stone beds, with the debris all over the yard, and choking the well. But that was about it. It was the bolt that had made more of its worrying first ever mark on the very Tavern. Here, vines were charred, and the stone seared on parts of the façade, and the roof, and the crucial chimney side. And the decorative Moon Star sign that had long been welded over the door, in the way it still traditionally squeaked, was a strawing of ash blown into the grooves of the stocky step and the cobbles.

'This shouldn't have happened.' Rhada frowned, in his full focus now. 'I must have the conductor checked without delay. The extreme gale could have got to the wiring, if it was unexpectedly low in other damage. Or, it could have been the thunder, likewise beyond the norm, that has rocked an imbalance in the inner relay mechanism.'

'Edrak will check it for you on his afternoon off today from the Institute.' Illana just remembered that happier item misplaced in both their darkened minds, as she stood with Rhada in the warming yard, tornly carpeted by wilting branches, twigs, and greenery. The woman had also been noting that there were no more bolt-related consequences to be seen, past the precincts of the Inn. There was no cinderised ground or vegetation. Nothing but the wind's work in this case, with a sorrowful series of not as strong spinney trees nearly thrashed to the riven grass, random saplings snapped, and de-bloomed hedgerows gouged out, or flattened in straggles, on their downwards twist to the indiscernible village.

'Ah, yes. Edrak will do that,' Rhada said, with his own happier refreshed memory, and his rush of fondness – nicer feelings on a morning of a minority of them – for the young student of science, with his personality as pleasant as his looks, shortly to be the son he'd never had. He had dearly wanted a son, but regretfully he and Illana had only been able to have Soletra. Not that his daughter wasn't the rosiest apple of his eye. 'And it would be doubly welcome today if he finally had news of a breakthrough in what they're attempting to do up there.'

'Do you think that will ever be?' sighed Illana, more of a doubter this day.

'Edrak serves the cleverest people at the Vaal Institute. People that wouldn't waste their mega brains and high value time on a truly hopeless project,' Rhada said.

But he had his equal doubts that morn concerning the dream of over a quarter of a century, and the ceaseless industry of the same duration, which had perpetually spotlighted the vener-able Institute of Technology. A huge fortress of a building in the next, more modern Sector that, with its finest laboratories and research facilities and its prime situation on the shielded Gratan elevation between the twin mountains, lured all Zalan's scientists of greatest acclaim.

At the age of 18, Edrak, of the respected Seran family, had been at the paragon of an Institute for three Summers. He had been apprenticed there to some of the scientists of renown, since leaving the leading University in the Southern Hemisphere's City of Spires. He loved it there. He was zealously dedicated to his yet lowly role in the enormous scheme of things, though it did involve him in that astronomical enterprise he stoically believed in, and had his cherished hopes of obtaining scientist status himself at a future date. Hopes that with his intelligence as considerable as his zeal, and the praise he rightfully earned from his mighty masters, had every likelihood of being fulfilled. Rhada, Illana, and Soletra had always been as proud of the commendable youth as his kindly, widowed mother, with whom he lived in a big, gabled cottage in the orchardlands at the other side of the valley.

Not long after this, Illana was letting Rhada get on with his outdoor fettling before the noon trade, and going to seek the inhabitually silent and retreative Solana that glum morning. She found the girl still at her chores. Soletra, somehow conniving to be externally calm over her growing hive of emotions inside, was tenaciously cleaning on a hearth copper just about where the sinister stranger had been leaning last night. The copper did seem more stubbornly pitted from the raindrops he had shed.

'Edrak will be well on his way, child. Off with you at once to wash and change!' Illana clucked and shooed like old Fayor's pet black hen, never guessing at Soletra's out of character grudge-edged reluctance and even pained remonstrance at the back of her fixed, sham smile.

When her husband had tidied the yard, and returned window

boxes and flower tubs, and she was baking fresh sater cakes, and concocting syrupy sweets for the first spring tourist shuttle due later in the afternoon, Illana told Rhada, 'It is good Edrak is coming. I still think that terrible traveller put a spell on Soletra more than the fear he put into us. And for all I wouldn't wish our daughter to know any of the shadow we are left with, I am starting to feel it could be healthier than dark bewitchment.'

Some of the noontide regulars arrived as Soletra, spruce in a long jade dress with short petal-shaped sleeves, was enthusiastically brushing her freely flowing hair to the lime luminosity of her eyes. This group of men consisted of those that had been at the Inn last night; they had come earlier than the others to see how Rhada had fared in the wake of their ignoble flight. They were as abashed and guilty as the Taverner, with his no recriminations for them. But neither were they any braver than him with the day. Especially when they had, furthermore, walked into the something left over from the night.

And after opening comments on thankfully no serious storm havoc for the village, just things badly blown, and on the communicated knowledge the storm had oddly only been in this region, the subdued fellows again unrestfully began discussing with Rhada the fabulous, frightening stranger. Re-introducing the topic Rhada had tried to mentally elbow aside, simply to discover desisted mention of the dark disrupter hadn't meant desisted thought.

Nonetheless, there was a ray of comfort for the Taverner, as was for them all, and that did lift a corner of the lingering room shadow dissuading the brunt of the sun. Today's main customer spokesperson, Hahn, who'd been a mute last night, now announced in no unglad or stinted terms that the star wanderer, with the name they never said, hadn't been seen anywhere near the valley and Kratana since his departure from the Inn. He seemed to have gone on his way, wherever that was to – with the drizzlingly damp blackness.

'Had he intended visiting us below, it would have been before now,' reckoned the beige-haired younger man, that sole daring one, for a batch of seconds, to address the coward-making individual. 'He should be miles from here instead.'

Rhada let himself indulge in that relief, and suggested they drink a toast to the riddance in the ale they wouldn't be boycotting any more, or the pipes they were lighting up.

'Somebody the likes of him would only be passing quickly on to grander places,' an older patron said through prompt tobacco haze for needfully robust puffs at his pipe. 'What would there be for him in a humble fistful of homes? He might not even have bothered about your Inn, Rhada, if he hadn't wanted to warm and dry at your fire.'

There were varitoned mumbles of agreement to that on the verge of the toast, somebody saying then, 'I can't get over it for the mazed life of me! His brazen disregard for the Zalan storm! His ridicule of the bolt almost.'

This induced a spate of louder annotation on, 'Only a madman would do that! But whatever he was, he was no madman.'

'Or a man with the ego of an omnipotent!'

'But it has to be still a brand of madness. To have no fear when the bolt is screaming right about you, with your dreadful end forecast in its circles of fire! No sentient being should be that unafraid.'

'No normal sentient being! And what was normal about

him? Not just mocking our storms from Galactic hell, but giving us the evil eye – inserting the fears in us, of the old, primeval kind.'

'And yet able to charm, as much as chill, innocent young girls. Be irresistible to them, more than alarming. Like the siren moons of K'toa…' That from Rhada, to silently recalling more sensitive nods and stares, no vocal allusion to his daughter.

Hahn just said, 'That could be the keyword, my friends. Whatever he is, more than who.'

The voice of Zalan superstition was rampant.

The Tavern talk had drifted up to Soletra with the pipe smoke and ale fumes. She listened hard to all that she could distinguish. Her brush strokes bridled, and a curl of her lip that wasn't her.

The remainder of the noon patrons showed in haphazard clusters, each expressing their share of the relief in antique clock chime echo, for the comparative sparing of their village in the worst ever storm, and with their unpleasant memory of it alone. But they were soon drawn into renewed recounting of that direful more than the storm they'd been favoured to miss. And although they hadn't seen the fantastic and fearsome roamer of the Cosmos, the unfading unnerve of the recounters was unslothfully conveyed to them. With the shadow in the room that wasn't from the rafters.

Soletra watched from the top of the stairs as Edrak walked through the door; his fit, youthful body moving in that quiet, unassuming style, claiming attention all the same. He was a striking lad in the continuing quiet and unpretension. He had a well-formed face, embellished by the clear bloom of his youth, the sky-blue glisten of gentle, sensible eyes, and the nicest mouth hardly without the smile that also flecked those eyes. And his teen half-braided hair was that rarer colour of Vratt metal brown, with streaks of gold in it, like from spun sunbeams.

He looked extra personable today, wearing an embroidered brown tunic trimmed with gold, plus a gold chain waist belt, to go illustriously with his hair. A lot of him was behind the big bouquet of star flares, prime Spring flowers, for Soletra.

That is, he looked extra personable to Rhada, Illana, and the customers, who welcomed him warmly and respectfully, and perhaps gratefully too that noon, when he carried a splash of his own sun transcending the real one into the room of wrong shadows. But to Soletra, standing there in rustling jade, Edrak was suddenly so pale, and puny, and barely alive, beside that dynamic image emblazoned in her head. That somebody who, with mind-shattering verve and intensity, lived beyond life, set it alight, and with the face of a mythical God in the glow of the red lightning eyes that could melt you into the ground, and marvellous, manly physique emitting the pulsant power to electrify your liquefaction.

And just as suddenly, the girl didn't want to spend the rest of the day with her eclipsed beau! To visit his cosy little home, have the cosy little supper with him and his darling of a mother, and later embark on the cosy little romantic stroll with him, watching the sun sink over the blue fells, and the moon sail out like a stately starship, the moon planet in vague, spectral tow.

She didn't want that. Not a modicum of it.

In ordinary circumstances she wouldn't have, couldn't have done it, if she had desired to. As kind and caring as she'd ever been herself. But today. Today, circumstances were starting not to be ordinary. Causing her not to be that kind and caring any more.

There was all that – diverse, and adverse, mostly indefinable – other inside her… Which she honestly didn't know what to do with. For all it seemed to know what to do with her.

Ordinarily, too, she could never have performed her small act with such cleverness to deceive. The bad headache that had come on all at once, making her feel sick and dizzy and unable to contemplate anything for a while, but her bed. Yet performed there she did, good enough to win a trophy. Everybody swallowed it whole without chewing. Edrak was sorry and disappointed, of course, but his boundless consideration took him over, and he was urging the 'sufferer', along with her similarly duped parents, to retire straight to that bed.

'I'll get to see you again as soon as I can, Soletra. I could maybe wangle the hi-speed mini shuttle for a brief hour,' he said, tenderly soft in his steadier pulse of a voice just lacking to her ears, as the sight of him to her curtained, craftier gaze.

Soletra gave more convincingly painful gestures, and strove not to criminally flinch when Edrak lovingly kissed her cheek.

Begging to be let be for the afternoon, Soletra re-climbed the stairs to her novel sloping room of lower beams and floral tapestry hung walls, tucked privately under the eaves. She did lie down on her gaily quilted bed by the arch window. She might not have had a headache. But she had more than sufficient going on within her.

Edrak didn't stay long. Only to have the snack Illana had insisted on getting him, and to examine the lightning rod for Rhada. Soletra plainly heard him and her father on the roof, with her room being near that part of the roof, and the window open a teeny notch.

'The wires are intact, sir. But some of them are getting a tad thin,' Edrak said to the Taverner. 'Not that I should have thought it was to the extent of allowing the bolt to come that close.'

'Well, it obviously was, lad,' Rhada replied. 'Had I known, I would have reactivated the prehistoric storm shutters as an added precaution.'

'Which were only substandard deterrents before the rods,' said Edrak. 'And are now only an interesting touch to the old-world décor. Anyhow, I'll reline the whole cable on my next longer time off.'

'I'm obliged to you. But I'd be more obliged if you could indeed bring that news of your boffin employers seeing light at the end of their ambitious project tunnel!'

'It will happen,' Edrak said, with his unflagging confidence. 'But a miracle like harnessing the forces of the Zalan bolt to convert them into astounding and lasting benefits for the Planet, can't be achieved overnight.'

'Try a few years,' said Rhada drily. 'But I suppose it could be too good to be true. Transforming a killer might bring immense advantages for Zalan, by providing inexhaustible, cheap and effortless energy for our power plants, and the kind of fuel to take our ships in an eye blink to far distant star systems, and their more prosperous trade lanes.'

'It will happen,' Edrak reaffirmed. 'And Professor Sanskril, the latest top scientist to Vaal, really may be that turner of the tide. I can't say much, but what he's been working on for months in the secluded West Tower laboratory, and which is something he has definite hopes about, could be nearer completion than he'd thought. He said this morning that the king of storms last night had brought him the king of brainwaves.'

'Oh. We could do with something spirit-raising out of that storm!' declared Rhada, with heavy significance. 'And I'm not just talking of murderous bolts with a capital M, or almost as murderous gales.'

'Then what, sir?' asked the alert Edrak.

'You won't have heard about it yet, will you? With being…' The voices were starting to get fainter, indicative of Edrak and the Taverner moving to climb down from the roof. And shortly, Soletra couldn't hear them at all.

The girl sat up with annoyance. She would like to have heard more of what they were saying there. What her father would say to Edrak about the sensational dark derider of that worst storm, and the unnerver of men. And what Edrak would say back.

When the pleasant youth had been waved off by her parents – Illana again thanking him for the flowers in her 'unwell' daughter's stead – Soletra, the new born deceiver, got up from her bed to sit at the window. She'd just had the absurd idea that the stranger, with the unspoken name constantly spoken with awed thrill in the darkening sacristy of her mind, wasn't on his way to enviable fresh pastures, but that he was coming right back to the Inn in this day after sunny calm. Coming to – see her. To keep the promise that had to have been! As she'd had the excited impulse to go watch for him.

She watched through the sun-speckled pane and the dancing of the Jennas outside it, those flying insect beauties with their colour changing wings.

She watched and watched all the afternoon, with a ready

flush on her palpitating cheeks, and an ecstatic heart.

But he didn't come.

He didn't come, when everybody else and their sister did, with the latest design tourist shuttle whirring in from the east.

And Soletra slumped towards the portals of silent distraction.

Chapter 5

DARKER DAYS FOR KRATANA IN THE VALE

Soletra dreamed of him that night, too. And they weren't dreams flavoured with her distraction. The very opposite. They were more wild and exciting, more reckless and uninhibited, the sensual and the erotic sown in and out with devious, darkling thread.

And they were so startlingly and disarmingly real.

She was in his arms that held her in a preciously crushing vice, and sublimely sawing volts of that electric of him. His eyes of their dark flame gloriously struck, singed, and consumed her to their menacingly secret depths. His fire ring-flashing hands caressed her with more live jolts. His voluptuously smiling mouth of unbearable allure pressed hotly and ignitingly, hungrily and insatiably on hers, devouring like his eyes, bringing her into eager learning and yearning. Letting her know what kisses truly were, and that she'd been bereft of them before – and how!

And then she was being swathed in black, shiny reams of that cryptic cloak, with its own depth to the shine, its warmly wet, slippery feel, and its strange, unfabric whisperings, and was being carried by him, her body feather-light on his burning

43

winds of passion. Soaring on them with him, going through spinning, exploding blood red stars to eerie, astounding, fearful places. Lost lands of sun and shadow, and phantom twilight in between, sinister and splendid horizons beyond terrains of whirlpooling and cascading coloured cosmic dust, and divine and disturbing, ever varying surreal-scapes in either dark-rimmed tantalise or brooding bidding.

The girl in fact woke in a soft mauve daybreak to feel in sweaty shivers and shakes that she had surely been with him. In his desirous and desirable arms, and taken by him to the farthermost, unexplored corners of the Universe, and all sorts of stellar heavens and hells.

And, not only that. As she sighed to the essence of her, and stretched to new heights and breadths, all those known and unknown things that had been invoked in the formerly ungauged deep of her, thrust themselves quite savagely further forth, and kindled themselves into the flames of him, to just about internally incinerate her. Things that were more recognisable, and more unrecognisable, which, while they felt threatening, alien, totally unright, forbidden, and profane, offered exalting joy, wonder, and unparalleled rapture. Off the scope of belief and conception.

Heavens and hells that could have come with her out of those dreams.

Rhada and Illana had dreamed of him again as well. But only more unadulterated nightmares. To give them no rest in their sleep.

And it was the same with that certain band of Moon Star regulars, who could no better get by the night of the storm, and Zaltar Valada. And with those who hadn't seen the stranger, yet had been grimly influenced by the ill accounts and iller 'tarryings' passed on to them. This included Edrak, in his room overlooking the technicolour orchards. Horrid black-cloaked, fire-emanating apparitions had pitilessly and perilously pursued the fine, upstanding young man through gloomful forest and glen, until the dawn bird of the fells had sung him awake.

Soletra laid longer in her bed that morning. She was at a bigger loss to know how she was to cope with the more drastic upheaval inside her, of what she could title and what she couldn't. Just how could she go on playing her sweet, serene self, keeping the violent vortex from the flat calm? But then, in some belongingly darkest miracle of an answer to that, as she gazed unseeingly at the strengthening sun painting her room gold, the latest poignant, painful surfeit of it all within her, surprisingly slowly modified. From there, gradually worming back into that newfound deep of her from whence everything had been as inexplicably summoned. Much in the way of night creatures fleeing the dawn for the ever dusk of the lairs.

And she knew what she could hide more easily.

And did. As early as breakfast, fooling her adoring parents into thinking she was their shy, docile Soletra again – perhaps a dot quieter – with all bewitchments gone like the bewitcher.

The girl was back to forgetting loyal, loving Edrak alto-gether, until by the futuristic communicator installed in features of the past, he concernedly wanted to know how she was that day. She was only willing to commit herself fully when he'd sorrily said he couldn't re-visit the Moon Star or home for another week, maybe more; implying events must be afoot at the Institute. Then, in her restrained satisfaction to a degree that should have amazed her, she assured him of her welfare.

She subsequently spent the remains of the morning and a large slice of the afternoon, heart hammeringly between her never more tedious chores, and her restored hope bolstered by her satisfaction about Edrak, tied with tighter strings to Vaal, to hear the sounds she craved to hear. That lively, dominant tread on the cobbles, and the whispering whoosh, and slimy slide of the curious cloak, that would take him through the Tavern door, not just her dreams.

It, alas, began to look like a bleak repeat of yesterday. Her futile and fruitless waiting that soon plummeted her back into despair. And desperation, now.

But he had promised her – hadn't he?

On her repose time, she was even frantically and foolishly impelled to slip out and seek him!

She traversed some distance in her desperation. She ran, and pantingly walked nearly all the scenic tourist track away from the valley. Going through kaleidoscope woods, over hump-backed bridges, up and down flowery slopes, by the legendary stile of the moon nymphs and the monolith, and 'seeing' pool of the pale Seer, until she was on the browsing brow of the carmine hillock, where you could glimpse the far cataract commune, and the old, grandfatherly mountains.

But all the agitated girl encountered were strolling outlanders viewing the sun-coaxed recovery of the resilient environment, piping birds of every invented colour, and insects that were mobile particles of glitter frosting the breeze of a thousand fragrances.

The stranger seemingly had gone with the storm.

Soletra trudged wretchedly home. There to face the

mellowing remains of the day, feeling trapped in a bedazzling nebula of conflicting lights and darks that had no way out, only the one irreversible way in. And then to know, with the advancing dusk and switching on stars, the deep, secret stirrings in her again, and the beckonings of those dreamscapes in their all, and more shadowy, thrills.

'I'm sure Soletra is quite pining for Edrak,' said Illana, when she'd packed her daughter to an early bed with a soothing Ooxan tisane. The woman spoke as she rearranged Edrak's flowers she'd mistaken Soletra's snubful attitude towards for sensitivity.

But Rhada wasn't really listening in his surprisingly un-alesome respite after designing a new sign. He was busily pondering upon what could possibly be on the go now at the Vaal Institute to call for days of every hand at the pump.

He might have been happier, had he known.

In that establishment, safely between the two mountains where low cloud climbed down their crags to wisp the steeply spearing laboratory towers, there was much more physical activity than usual. Impregnable walls resounded to everybody hurrying about their new or accelerated industries in scarcely suppressed excited hopes and anticipation. It was only that momentous late evening when there was a lull, and that was rife with all the excitement bursting forth into amazement, and all the hopes and anticipation into first born exultation.

Edrak couldn't believe it, as he stood with others of the team in Professor Sanskrill's private experimental chamber, and gaped at the astonishing enigma of a contraption the prominent scientist had been working on virtually non-stop.

The machine had been practically finished in yesterday's spurt of monumental inspiration resulting from that viler storm.

There were just the proverbial few loose ends, Sanskril proclaimed. The bespectacled, moon-faced, haystack-haired fellow nearly rubbed his never greater skilled hands with glee over what he was at last exhibiting to his well-qualified colleagues and their devoted young servitors. Many of these had been slavishly involved in this mammoth project for countless years before his prestigious advent, during which time servitors had become adept scientists themselves.

This man, yes, a shining light in the brain fest, and the internationally heralded and baptised best hope of the era and its germinated objective of wildest aspirations and vast improbabilities, went invigoratedly on to his boggle-eyed, slack-jawed, thrilled audience,

'Painstaking tests will begin tomorrow, and will continue solidly until the apparatus is ready for the ultimate one. On the bolt, itself.'

Edrak swallowed on eager, irregular breaths, and down to his same heart poundings. But as his lit blue eyes reverently absorbed the structure in front of him, that was decidedly peculiar and bizarre, and yet somewhat awful in aspects, he prematurely tasted the dish of long, tenaciously striven-for, and often dubbed impossible, supreme success.

The Bolt Catcher looked precisely just that.

Sanskril, talking to his most promising pupil later when the scientific genius had done revising his electron menu for the first test, said, 'Edrak. If all is successful, it would also prove, or disprove, Dr Quent's pet theory about the bolt. That it is the one fireball only every time in its term of the tempest, which simply regenerates, not the perpetual new birth of the many—'

'With respect, that idea is a bit far-fetched, Sir,' Edrak replied, diffidently basking in being singled out by the big man, and no longer the green novice who'd thought forcefields were a defence against the bolt, when it just voraciously fed on the likes. 'And it would lessen the benefits. The one bolt per storm.'

'One bolt per storm, as you droly put it, would still keep us ahead. The power in it to regenerate,' smiled Sanskril. 'But Quent can be a lot far-fetched in his wisdoms. And, as you know, I can't warm to the theory.'

The latter, that was always enough for Edrak, but the youth did wonder then, would a recharging bolt be more comforting, or not?

The storm alarmingly came again that night! Yet it never came twice within six rounds of the moon – sufficient thanks for that! And again, it broke unforecasted in tranquil star shine, and inexplicably only in the Kratana region; the belated local sirens a lost cause in the instantaneous loud, valley-quaking crashes of thunder.

There was no gale tonight, not a breathlet of wind. And the rain was on and off, incorporating drizzle, and the sky's floodgates opened. But to the clamour of the thunder never letting up at all, and from the now sixty-pronged lightning, the born faster bolt was, if anything – and it could be – more ferocious than the last supposedly worst time.

Not that the Tavern wasn't somehow spared tonight of the petrifying proximity of the small wheel of flame. Even with a likely defective rod. The village had its turn instead. The screaming red demon shot sizzlingly about the valley for every extended minute of the storm, and got too close to the artistic huddle of antique habitations, enough to strike sparks from singularly struggling roof rods here, and simulate the Madra Festival fireworks.

The Proprietors of the luckier Moon Star were, however, also nearly as relieved that there had been no other repetitions, like sudden dictatorial, impatient bangings on the door! Though Rhada and Illana had disagreeably imagined it into nervously half expecting it. And Soletra, longing for that in an agony of suspense, was to flounder back into despair.

The disquieting reports were soon to be had from Kratana that next day. All in another lurid, depressing aftermath of the phenomenon of the unheard-of second storm scraping at the heels of the one before, and with more wrath yet; both only in the valley district.

No. There was still remarkably small damage to the village. The roof rods had mustered, narrowly, with surveyors of scorched walls, and chimneys, and spark pitted slates, speculating as Rhada had on the vicious gale of the other storm having upset the wiring. And it was the same with the environmental rods, only the rather more charcoaled trees, bushes, and stretches of earth beyond their scope. But there had been something else – along that different, shadier avenue of fear.

In the middle of the storm there had been a loud knocking on the door of the last cottage on Salen Street, the home of Di-Grell, the custodian of the Mill and Wheel. And it had been perforcedly opened to a lone traveller in dramatic eddies of slippery black cloak, and with long red hair rivering vibrantly into another hellish night.

The Star Wanderer had not gone on his dark way.

He had also familiarly compelled them to admit him – the custodian, his wife and family, ranging from tots to teens to give some of those who hadn't seen him yester-eve, a baleful example of him. Of his strange, stunning attraction, his sardonic arrogance and scorn, and his perilous powers which counted among them that sorcerous prowess to both unnerve and mesmerise, terrify and enchant, bringing shadow of the old matters, with the unlocking gates to the darkly wondrous new. All they could have done without.

He had again disruptively sheltered, with mulled wine pressed on him by those he could make uncharacteristically grovel. The exception was Loriste, Di-Grell's eldest daughter, receiving the brunt of his wizardry of charm; her parents more lax in fear than Soletra's, having failed to remove her from the terrible fellow. And again, he had stayed, drinking in reactions more enjoyably than the wine, until the abrupt conclusion of the storm, when he had swept off blackly and malevolently, amidst the whirling, whispering cloak.

Only, on this occasion he hadn't left alone.

He had been followed by the beautiful and bewitched Loriste, who'd got through the door before it could be shut or she be stopped, the girl running possessedly into the wet, chillier night with only her thinnest leisure robe on.

Di-Grell, jogged out of his torpor, had sprinted distraughtly after her, but to no avail. He couldn't catch a glimpse of billowing violet hair and white gauzy skirts.

The night, with its burns healing in the scraps of rain, had swallowed Loriste up with the stranger.

The panicking custodian had thumped on neighbours' doors for assistance, and in fraught minutes a braver party of painedly understanding fathers had been dispatched with him to find the runaway. But for all they had searched the whole night and morning, they had still met with no trace of the girl.

Nor the stranger they weren't as happy about.

'It's like she has vanished from the surface of the Planet,' said the relater of the worrying tale to Rhada. 'Along with – him. Whether or not they be together…'

'May they not be!' Rhada wished, to a shudder on a shudder, and he bluntly declared what was in everybody's darker coloured minds. 'The man is a fiend!'

'Well. Only a fiend could have effects like that on honest, decent folk. And their innocent, trusting daughters.'

'But they will go on searching, yes?' said Rhada, with his resolute guard of Soletra working to a pitch. Soletra, as ever, was secretively listening to all this.

'Di-Grell will search every inch of our World, if needs be. And many of us will search with him. In the meantime, the devil take his own back! Wherever Loriste is, he spellbound her, as he brought fears old and new to others, and lured her from the safety of her home.'

'Aye. The devil take him back!' growled another feeling father.

As Soletra did listen, her face was flushed and her eyes unblinking in their feverish gleam. Her hands were clenched to, the nails cutting into the palms enough to extract blood. In her was no horror for the story told, or any consternation for her friend Loriste. Not at all. She was just knowing a passionate self-anger and hurt, and a bitterest envy and remorse, for not daring and doing as Loriste had. For not going after him, too. Following him into the night. To be with him. Where she herself had no doubt her hated rival in ascendance would be.

As for hearing that glamorous, mystical man of all men said to be a fiend, a sort of monster. To her, it only added to the splendour and deadly fascination of him, and the torments of her envy and regret.

It definitely didn't ease or appease the transformed girl, when Rhada laid down his stringent rules for a daughter never more precious to him. Rules that were to confine her to the house and supervised inches of the yard, until these latest shocking incidents were resolved. If ever, and however they would be.

The dreadful tidings came only the next day.

Loriste hadn't disappeared without a trace. She had just gone farther than the tireless searchers had looked. Than they had thought she could be.

She was in the purple forest, massing their miles of mist and dew into mountain country.

She was slumped lifelessly across knobbly tree roots groping out of the turfy ground. Sheeny leaves were on her cotted spread of hair, and on her poor thin robe twirled damply around her. And overhead, the purple forest birds seemed to sing a sorrier song. There wasn't a mark on her. Only the expression frozen onto her corpse pallor of lost senses and no hope any more.

The local physician sighingly proclaimed she had died from exposure. Affirming no human hand laid on her. This led to the belief that Loriste hadn't been able to catch up with the stranger; his lively, long-legged strides could have put him well ahead of her at once, taking him and his direction into the cover of darkness. And that the frantic girl had just forged blindly on, maybe calling to purposely, or not, deaf ears, until she had somehow got as far as out here, and had been overcome by the weariness from a defeat as frenzied, with the sustaining heat of her haste lapsing into the killing cold.

She had perished in a frenzy of aching despair. Falling into her untimely, eternal sleep, under the raddled boughs of the old trees that wept those leaves on her.

The evil entrancer of a man could only be indirectly blamed for the tragedy. But anger and resentments rode high and hard on the general grief, even if such spiked emotions to spur the adrenaline could still never replace the nameless fear of him. And the superstitious awe.

Everybody, instead, had it passed forthwith as an iron-clad village law. That on no account for the foreseeable future was any door in Kratana, or out of it, to be opened in a Zalan storm.

All but one person mourned the sad death. Soletra, ever more not Soletra, didn't lend herself to sorrow for a girl she'd closely known. Or repent of the envy and ill will she'd felt towards her these two days. It was the deplorable opposite. Beneath her holding outer calm, she harboured the cruel joy and triumph that Loriste hadn't overtaken the stranger that night, and had been an eliminated rival in the process. From then onwards, she lived with a new placating reliance upon a promise that could still be kept.

Chapter 6

BOLT OF THE HUNDRED-PRONGED LIGHTNING

The third anomalous storm at sedated night and in that one vicinity, was a week or so after the plight of Loriste. Just when everybody was starting to breathe easier; the former two storms in their unbeforeknown quick succession seeming to subscribe to a solitary freakish event.

With twice the alarm for the mistake, and for more than the storm, and the nurturing abnormality of its frequency getting not a little serious, doors were barred to the hilt. And in carbon copy of Rhada, all the olden-day shutters reactivated to give that added protection, a morsel better than none.

But there were no knockings for admittance anywhere that night. Nobody came out of the storm in his sanguine shroud of cloak, and his darker aura of peril.

The Zalan bolt was the sole terror then. Never less requiring anything to implement it. From what got to be an astoundingly awful, hundred-pronged lightning redly ripping up the sky, with no record of this likes either in the written history of the Planet, the bolt was twice the fiery demon. A more enraged and ferocious force than ever. Its destructive qualities reached a whole new high, and still more particularly and almost supernaturally now for the tiny valley village. Many a roof rod was flamingly fused, reduced to smoking metal melting in chimney stone, and a couple of cottages were struck, collapsing in the bolt's crimson kindlings. The rain, the only mercy, was doused, and there were some nasty injuries for the inhabitants, along with a single fatality – Lacto, the oldest standing villager. Many of the environmental rods were fused, too, with more than a few of these melting into the tree, bush, and ground for the verdure to be incinerated clean away, and the earth charred bare, split, and broken, with the rain to make smokier black mires of it.

Unanswerably, and almost supernaturally, the Moon Star Tavern had once more remained unscathed – just one completely spared site at the head of the assaulted vale. The oddly-favoured building, however, was to later be a haven of relief for the hurt and temporary homeless. Not that Rhada was any further consoled. There was a bigger, and worse, problem brewing. Even to supersede the evil stranger who had to be gone this time.

'I pray last night was still only on the rare agenda of freak-ish,' Rhada palely said to his wife. 'If not, and the bolt isn't playing at fluke but is suddenly somehow beginning to prove invincible against our rods, how can any of us be safe?'

'Well. Why can't Nature have a freakish spell? Rasher moments as it's never had before? Like all of us,' Illana laboured to convince him. And herself.

Rhada just shook his head with anxious perplexity, missing, as Illana did, Soletra stealing out of the room. The girl, with her new soft, sly stealth, and her more shadowy green eyes that looked cravingly beyond a storm of fresh dread propor-tions, and village refugees dolorously converging on the Inn in fraggy clumps from the scorched and swampy ways.

'How I wish Edrak could be bringing cheerier news from the Institute on this day, above any,' Rhada soliloquised on prolonged head shakes. To silence on that front, with the young man getting his no concessionary visits yet, or much airwave time, when he kept Vaal counsel, and spoke only of his solicitude for a said quieter Soletra wearing a brave face.

But had the Taverner known it, progress was marching on nicely at that establishment in the brindled mountains.

All loose ends relating to that hopefully revolutionary machine had been satisfactorily tied, with some valuable input from Edrak earning him Sanskril's thrifty praise. And the tests were about to begin.

'It cannot be too soon!' exclaimed the celebrated scientist-in-chief. 'If for presently utterly incomprehensible hows and whys, the bolt is indeed developing a new terrible potential.'

'It is also exceedingly peculiar, Sir, and not unperturbing itself, that this is all happening only in the Kratana area of our Sector,' Edrak said, gazing more dependably than ever upon the incredibly fantastic, ingenious, and untoldly complex metal spectacle sheering its good 16 feet before him. 'The new worrying power, and so unnatural rapid sequence of the storms.'

'I do have Professors Dralt and Toa on that investigative detail already. But I can acquit no other minds, and my own, until the absolute success of my machine is assured.'

'Certainly not, Sir. Especially now, your brilliant invention has to take priority over everything.'

'Yes. It is the solution to be procured before the cause,' said Sanskril, adding sympathetically, 'but, again, I am sorry about your village having to suffer. You haven't been that fortunate at all lately at Kratana, have you? What with the storms, and that poor girl beguiled to her death.'

'That was unspeakable about Loriste.' Edrak never liked to dwell on it, or on how it could have been his Soletra.

'I'm pleased, though, that your mother is alright. With your outlying home just getting a blackened wall,' Sanskril said, his condoling end to more sympathetic noises. 'And that she'll be moving in with her in-laws-to-be at the sounder Inn, while the crisis is on.'

Edrak was pleased to his noble, sensible soul about that. All his loved ones under the same, trustiest roof at this trying time. And he couldn't wait for the testing to start on what had to be the answer to the true and lasting safety of those loved ones.

Sanskril, consigning his honed dagger brain to another, more crucial phase in the proceedings, ordered the machine to be carefully wheeled on its retractable runners to the relevant chamber.

The Moon Star's noon patrons today were comprised of the regulars least afflicted by the latest worst storm. But the Tavern's rafters rang with their loud, concerned talk which the corpulent landlord soon participated in, his strained baritone with the other, varied tense timbres.

'Three storms that close. And each having got impossibly worse.'

'Yes. To a hundred-pronged lightning. And a bolt of new terrifying powers. It isn't right.'

'It's all just against the law of nature!'

'And the storms are never in the day now. Which is off

norm itself.'

'To me, it's more off norm that only this one region in our whole Sector is getting them. It's as if the bolt is waging war with us alone.'

'That's nonsense, Adran. You could be saying the bolt has a brain! It's all freakish of the first order, as Rhada sees it.'

'It could have had a brain last night! Its strikes were almost strategic in its extra fury.'

'You're letting this addle your wits. It just struck indiscriminately to me, with its two hells blaze.'

'Whatever. They'll no doubt be looking into things at the Institute. Rhada. How are they going on with that secret business of years to sort our bolt blight? We could do with encouraging news now.'

'Edrak doesn't tell me much, as he can't. But what he does impart isn't discouraging.'

'We can't take many more storms like last night. We were lucky that homes got more damaged than folk, and that there was only one death – old Lacto, his frail heart giving when the chimney went.'

'Ah. Poor Lacto. Was he on borrowed time.'

'Poor Lacto.' That from many sorrowful murmurs.

'That's two deaths we've had in a short spell.'

'But young Loriste wasn't killed in the storm.'

'She was in kind. By that madman who came out of it again!'

'Do you not think it is also odd? That he – whoever he is, and wherever he may be from, it could be best not to know – has only shown himself the twice he has, in a storm?'

'He has, hasn't he!'

'Wherever he can be from, he must be one of those storm-chaser fanatics. He has all the barefaced arrogance, audacity, and ego!'

'Nobody chases our storms! Intentionally courts a fiery destruction with the Zalan bolt. Even the most arrogant, audacious, and egotistical. Or the most foolhardy.'

'But a madman, as Termault just said, as we all have, very well might.'

'My friends. Let us discuss the storms, not the stranger. Attempt to figure how, in case – the Heavens forbid – they persist with this wrong regularity and force, we can protect ourselves against them, until the boffins can step in with answers and a cure.'

'Wisely spoken, Rhada. That is of the importance. Anyway, why the fixation on the stranger any more, when he has plainly gone now? But how can we defend against that fresh, devastating power?'

'That is so, Rhada. How! Our rods, that aren't defective after all, are starting to become as useless as the bewhiskered shutters!'

'We must put our heads together, and pool our ideas. We aren't scientists, but we're not unintelligent men. And it is doing something, or endeavouring to. Not sitting about helplessly, in subjection already.'

Soletra, the ever-unseen eavesdropper as she polished unnecessarily outside the bar room, had to silently scoff at the pathetic 'not unintelligent men', and she wasn't exempting her father. But she was more rankled about and distinctly smarted from the glued insanity label on a refulgent prince of the night, who was just sky high above other mortals, making them defunct, and, yes, half dead at the side of him.

She could actually easily want some of them quite dead! Like parents that nothing short of imprisoned her with their rigid restrictions. And a simpering wimp of a fiancé-to-be, that could have her drown herself in the mill race!

Chapter 7

'WATCH FOR ME IN THE STORM.'

The girl was still, and more ventfully polishing, when her mother called to her to turn her sedulousness kitchenwards.

Illana asked Soletra to pack her numerous batches of oven cakes into baskets to be delivered to the recovering villagers below that still had their homes, and the emergency repair workers on the guttered cottages of those that hadn't.

'My baking won't go to waste in the end,' Illana said, scurrying about on her nerves, and with smudges of flour unobviously on her paler plump face. 'But it makes me fret here, too, that they've cancelled the big shuttle trip because of our all-at-once appalling weather conditions. One cancellation, and others could follow, and that wouldn't bode well for our tourist trade.' And on and on she rambled, her tongue astride nerves also, until the arrant silence of her daughter penetrated her keyed-up chatter. Soletra was dutifully filling baskets in her calm, with none of her low boiling thoughts and feelings to be squandered on the needy of Kratana.

'Have you nothing to say, Soletra? Of such calamities?' Illana declared.

'Will it help to say anything, Mother?' Soletra replied cannily and callously coolly under her controlled quiet.

'Maybe it won't, child,' Illana just sighingly owned, blinder than ever to malicious changes right in front of her. As much as Rhada was.

She returned on her sigh to the traditional squat, sepia, bulbously-legged oven, disguising its ultra-modern performance, to take out the last of the speckled tan cakes. 'But it doesn't do to bottle it all up, either. You know, I think it would be wiser if I sent you to cousin Hildren's in her distant Sector. Just for the while – and she would love to have you.'

'No!' That had to be wrenched with more emotion from Soletra's pinched lips.

'I agree she can be a trifle finicky, and old maidly. But she has a heart of gold, and she does live within quick access to the Ocean World Sector. Remember, Soletra, all those astonishing floating mountain chains, and forests, silver and glass cities, and country hamlets additionally harvesting the sea for their water feature wonders.'

'No, Mother. I'm staying.' Soletra crumbled a cake in her harsher hands.

'And I understand. You won't want to be leaving Edrak. For all we're seeing precious little of him at this time.'

Soletra could have laughed at that, with spiteful scorn. She only restrained herself with maximum effort, and was glad in her disdain, and malice, of her father's tense, troubled head bobbing jarringly round the door to coincidentally proclaim Edrak's mother had arrived with her bags.

'I intended checking on her room again.' Illana trayed piping hot cakes, and wiped floury hands on her apron. 'She must have every comfort.'

'The room is fine.' Soletra snapped her head aside, and

bit down on her lip. Her annoyance was fiercely back at the coming of the widow Seran to lodge at the Inn. Yet not long ago she would have been overjoyed in all her affections for that kindest and mildest of women.

As soon as her pestilent packing was done, and she'd connived an exit from the kitchen, and an evasion of Edrak's mother, Soletra couldn't wait the tip of a second more to be on her own. On her own to freely think about him at last. And her latest, queer dream… To freely feel the all, and the whatever – connected with them both.

She even peremptorily violated the sticking, strict house rules, wangling herself outside, as far as the very banned Xylax shaded back gate, with its perfect seclusion she'd avariciously sought from people who'd been around her in hectic profusion since she'd risen that morning. In the indigo shelter of copious Xylax foliage that damply rustled above her, Soletra could without question unprohibitedly think… and feel… which was fervently, and feveredly, and agonisingly, driving her farther out of her mind. And then in the throes of it all, she mused upon that dream – so different to any of the incessant others – which she'd had last night, the night of the bolt at its new zenith. It had only been a shorter dream, and not one hosting the sinfully wild, sweet erotica of establishing habit, to transport her to those forbidden Cosmic Edens, but the realism of it had been greater than anything before, making it more in the calibre of a visitation for her in a sleepily waking moment.

He had appeared wraith-like inside her window, in the loneliness of her night. When the only storm had been in her, and he'd dimmed the one proper into a cessation for them. He had stood motionlessly there, in his red and black resplendence, his flame pour of hair in swelling waves of dazzle, and the ebony cloak now more strangely fitting to him like it was getting to be another, slimy skin. And there he had stayed, never moving nearer to her, with his figure flooringly re-apparent for the uncannily metamorphosing cloak. He had just looked at her, watched her intensely, with his eyes mocking, lureful red slits hazardously hotter live coals for her to be frazzledly raked over, and his snakily sneering, slyer, seductive smile.

Nor had he spoken but for that once, just before he'd as wraithfully vanished again. And it was only a few words then, his lips parting in their sneer and their sorcery, to slowly, softly, sibilantly slide them across the tauntingly kept space between them. Words that had their strangeness, too, and yet a mode of sense not in dream trend, and that were to be indelibly burned in her head as the paramount picture of him.

'I said we would meet again, little pretty. And we will. You could finally be the one. To face it, and not choose to be no more. Watch for me in the storm.'

But puzzle over those words and that hopefully darkly divine dispensation, as she could here in the conducive solitude, if no peace, she wasn't any more enlightened. Only knowing a dark faith in, and a dark reliance upon, a fourth night of the tempest, however gone past bad to the bone.

Chapter 8

A STRANGE DISCOVERY AT VAAL

'The initial tests are as successful, if not more than we had expected. We can now proceed with the remainder of them outdoors.' Sanskril announced it, with his fullest dose of satisfaction containing the hints of early major triumph. 'Edrak, relay my orders for the machine, and the attached trial conductive cables, to be taken immediately to the parapet on the north tower.'

'Yes, Sir! Rightaway, Sir!' Edrak, having watched agog with roof-hitting excitement and suspense the hitchless testings for hours of his mentor's famous fastidiousness, hurried to obey, half tumbling over himself with eagerness. Other vyingly excited apprentices and many of the scientists bunched unsegregatedly and loquaciously around Sanskril; a number of the scientists pencil-breakingly jotting down notes in well-thumbed pads.

Edrak delivered the message to the elite Transferral Unit, with the labourers in tow, enlivening eyes and tread there, and returned along the delaying gauntlet of accostals from workers of all departments in that quarter, to the side of his master, and Vaal's genius, nearly in lights. Sanskril had dismissed the youth's fellow apprentices in their noisier exuberance, and was listening non-committally to his colleagues, Latus and Brel, bandying last minute corrections to do with the final processing of their joint contribution to the planet's greatest project. The genuine, miles-long, self-sinking, self-running linkage cables.

Edrak said respectfully, 'If the outdoor testing is as successful, Sir, will the machine then really be ready?'

'To go into deadly serious action? To be lastly tested on the spot, so to speak? It will, Edrak. It will be directly transported to your area and its highest, flattest point, Dallan-Torrin plateau, and there speedily set up, luckily before any more of your riddlesome storms that are next on our probe list.

'By the way, after the exterior tests I do have to be optimistic about,' the Professor added, as Edrak stood on bigger, tensely thrilled springs, 'you can take the mini shuttle to the Moon Star, cheer them all with the hopeful news they will never have been more desperate for, and have a deserved rest until we have prepared the machine for its lengthier, but safer, overland journey tomorrow.'

'Sir. That is wonderfully kind of you!' Edrak couldn't credit, his ears echoing with test hummings and dronings yet. 'I don't know how to thank you.'

Sanskril shrugged that off and instead, shrewdly and as nearly wonderfully, asked the more illuminated youth his opinions about the computerised, endurable, malleable metal cablings, in turn linkable with the main power lines, that were being conferred on behind them.

Edrak was only too pleased and honoured to accommodate this man of outstanding intellect on an issue demanding its own importance in the super scheme. And his quietly submitted views were as sensible and sagacious as ever, supported by admiring approval, in reference to the special and revolutionary cables, that would for centuries unite the machine with the Jorran Dia, the massive power plant for both sectors. Certainly, to his promising mind, the competence of the cabling couldn't be improved upon by its authors.

Edrak felt hungrier for the overdue snack he'd been ordered to have in the required hour between two of the tests on the machine in the high open. His appetite had waned of late, with his magnified worries and fears for his dear ones back home. But today, with the advance on scientific dreams going at a tangent, and maybe his quick visit to them, where they were still safe in a tavern that seemed blessed holding each of them, he could tackle the tasty repast before him.

He was just tucking into twirls of seed bread seeped in honey butter when he was approached by Krael, his closest friend at the Institute and in this sector. The affable, slim, tan-haired youth of Edrak's age was employed in another department on the east wing. He was a second-year student in Vaal's computer-run agricultural and environmental division. Edrak thought that Krael, who often debonairly devised his own break, would be curious to his grinsome teeth about final bolt catcher information, not any the more available to him, and was primed with the titbit that the stable Sanskril could be bordering on dancing the dreva round the establishment! However, it was Krael soon turning the curiosity on him, with what he had foremost in his more jovially scholar's head.

'You know that, as a favour in my spare time, I've been looking up old data on what used to be the main computer,' he said to Edrak, the one he also envied in the nicest way for having a girl like Soletra: his Miss Right was as elusive as the

Morona Miasmas. 'And a relic it is!'

'For Professor Krrosan and his new archives hobby. Yes.' Edrak licked sticky fingers.

'Well,' said Krael, sitting on the table's edge, ignoring plates it was his custom to merrily filch from. 'I've accidentally come upon some pretty intriguing stuff, dating from a century or so ago, which must have been filed away, by mistake or meddling, in the primitive land tilling section, and has laid there ever since. As forgotten as all that old trivia.'

'Intriguing, how?' Edrak asked with pricked-up interest.

'The first piece was to do with sudden, extra capricious weathers at the tip of the eastern hemisphere. Just there. Near about the period of the Moon Planet's orbital shift of that decade. Various regions along the great Vracht Promontory were particularly affected, being plagued in turn by very, very bad storms. They didn't occur as preternaturally frequently as the ones recently in your little province, and rods didn't fail – though they struggled – but buildings and vegetation got a bit grilled, as folk got a lot alarmed. Thinking this could perhaps be helpful to the giga brains when they started probing with a vengeance into your storm peculiarities, I therefore clicked onto the rest of it, and – you'll never guess what I discovered next?'

'I won't, if you don't tell me,' Edrak said good humouredly over his fuelled interest.

'Take more of a bite out of this than your lunch! If it didn't happen that in the aftermath of three storms, all at a middling while from each other, there was disappearance and death. A girl for every village in those certain three areas, and of the age between 16 and 17! Similar to the girl at your Kratana.'

'What!' exclaimed Edrak, going straight as a lath in his chair.

'I said it was intriguing. But listen on. All the girls ran from their homes in the abating; vanished like they'd never existed, puzzling the searchers, and then were eventually found in some far forest or gully – dead of exposure and shock!'

'Gracious! This is fearfully amazing!'

'Isn't it? I've had that snip of documentation copied, too. So that at first chance you can read it for yourself, and Sanskril, and his top cranium cronies.'

Edrak emphatically nodded. 'But tell me more, Krael,' he said, when he'd surprisedly digested it, along with the honeyed bread. 'Was there any mention of a strange traveller being around at the time of the tragedies there?'

'No. The focus was only on the girls, and their identical, illogical behaviour signposting to their deaths. But Edrak. Wasn't that all way back? In another century? Your mystery stranger, I admit, from your description – secondhand, as it was – gives me the creeps, but would hardly have been on the scene then!'

'Of course not! What am I saying!' Edrak re-exclaimed to that prize example of folly.

'But it's all still the strangest coincidence, uh?' said Krael.

'Oh. It's that alright,' said Edrak, slower. 'For more girls like Loriste disappearing, and dying, after specifically bad storms. For all they were obviously never as bad as the storms we've been just having. These have been the worst in recorded memory. I shall love to hear what Sanskril says about your findings, when his mind is freer.'

'And I'm with you!' Krael heartily concurred. 'In the

interim, I might delve deeper into what's stored in that ugly old has-been.'

Chapter 9

DESTRUCTION!

The cone-shaped, lunar, metal mini shuttle left the Vaal Bay, ducking deftly out from under the long canopy of lit launching lights. With a soft whistle to it, like the breath of the rising moon wind it rode upon, with the moon pearl insects, the 'Star Racer' sped iridescently through the last of the sunset fires as they were being extinguished by the blue and purple smoke of the banking dusk clouds. Farther more purpling south, the neat, fleet vessel swung smoothly off the Vaal traffic lanes, and zoomed the faster towards the Quatran Circle – an ancient ring of white stone obelisks half as tall as the standard ship flies. Passing these, stroked with stubby fingers of purple-black shadow, the shuttle as deftly skimmed the darkening multi-coloured range of the high floral hills of S'lar, and dived with the grace of a fishing bird to go low over the gentler, twilit slopes, with their viridescent, mossy streamlets, and the smudgily darker forests, where waking night blooms were a thousand pinpricks of phosphorescence.

Still, Edrak, the expert pilot from Cruiser Captain tuition, could not get quick enough to his sector, and the tavern on the blue ridge. Not when he ached to see his loved ones after he hadn't for days impersonating months. And he was also the bearer of that new hope at the finish, to lighten their lives become as shadowed as the hills and vales below.

The outdoor tests on the Bolt Catcher, re-christened the Valadrian, had all been a success, and everything bode well for that ultimate test – in the field. The success of which here would add Primax 1 to the new name (Bolt Catcher, Nemesis 1), and be then instantly broadcast to all the Zalan governments, in this quadrant the ten wise men of Ladra, and after all the populations on the planet.

Edrak, passing an oncoming larger shuttle with the sociable flicking of nose lights between them, had, before his gratefully embraced flight, witnessed Professor Sanskril – maybe destined to be pedestalised as a universal scientific hero – presiding over the many preparations for the mammoth moving of the priceless machine. It had to be ready to be transported with the dawn to the subdued realms of Kratana and Dallan Torrin, the plateau once the nesting ground of an extinct, exceptional bird, that could be writing a fresh page in Zalan history. The machine would be having a lengthier journey, too, with it going overland by the slowest speed rail shuttle, but it wasn't to be risked by air, with the faster pace and adverse pressures that would upset the eggshell balance of super sensitive mechanisms. And even by snail train, there were endless precautions. Like the Valadrian being clamped down in a special, sealed, steel container welded to the engine, with Sanskril and his top men travelling inside to keep a vigilant eye on it every drawn-out inch of the way; Edrak, other skilled apprentices, and labourers, would be with the stouter attachments in following reinforced carriages.

It had also been pleasingly witnessed by all in the dream

that Sanskril, hither and thither in his critical overseeing, had been more optimistic than ever, clearly envisioning to those rubbed hands and two-year-old step, and making everybody else do it, a Primax 2, 3, 4, and on, and on. Victorious mass production! To serve every corner of the planet. Bring it, and every living thing on it, into a new Golden Age.

Edrak felt cheered enough by his Professor, never enheartening idly, to take on the chin his rationed time at the Moon Star, and mainly with Soletra, who his adoring gaze was deprived of these days. It wouldn't pull as intolerably at him when he had to get back to Vaal for that dawn, and his continuing role in that dream to make everything worthwhile, and which could be as close to being realised as the next storm, now much awaited by the scientist faction.

And, anyhow, wasn't it another cheering thought, all the liberty that would be had – with the miracle? Holidays aplenty would be awarded to everybody who had worked so hard and unyieldingly –many for years – on the project. From the king brain Sanskril, though he would be raring to press on with solving the erratic weather pattern, to the paltriest labourer, who wouldn't.

The youth's spirits lifted at the sighting of familiar landmarks, denoting arrival on the far-flung outskirts of Kratana. But they took a tumble again when he flew lower over his blistered home, dejectedly deserted in blackened orchards, and over the more severe damage in the village, that was the quicker revealed for trees felled by flame. He sighed heartfully for all this, shaking his gold and copper head, and letting the Star Racer waver in its smoothest course.

It all brought back as well what his friend Krael had dug

up on that relic of a computer. The old and new question mark of after-storm disappearance and death. He hadn't forgotten any of it. He couldn't. It was that bewilderingly strange, and freshly not quieting. But his mission of real hope for those dear to him had heaved it behind until the darkly fitter moment.

'It is the queerest thing, for sure,' Edrak said to himself, before repeating his sigh at that grand 'antique' of a mill and wheel only as blackened earth, or black dust blown on heat drunk water. He was about to stretch his sigh at the roofless worship house, exhibiting its shrivelled, crumpling interior, for it just to be whipped clean away from him in dislocating strands.

That was when the lightning struck again tonight from a threatless, silvering sky, turning everything red, like the world spilling its blood. A jagged prong separating from the thirty of them already, and heading right for Edrak. A daggering missile of crimson fire that could have had a look of intent.

Astoundingly and terribly, the single shaft did its worst without the others, or the unformed bolt, cutting through the supposedly invulnerable shields of the shuttle easier than a knife through honey butter, blazing a hole in the hull of the fairly resistant Moon Planet ore, and searing in twain the air aglimmer with instrumentation. The sizzling prong missed Edrak by a bristling hair-breadth, frying the controls the shock had jerked him aside from, but causing no ignition.

It was all so typically sudden, the youth didn't have chance to cry out. He plunged speechlessly with the Star Racer and its now unhealthy fractured whine, to the ground beneath. The craft scraping past the last cottage tops that had survived the best, and ploughing into the still heavily soaked earth, which minimised impact to the prevention of break-up, or fire here from the fuel tanks. The Racer mounded and caterpillared the miry soil and dissected vegetation, and throefully shuddered to a stop half in and out of it all.

It had scarcely finished shuddering when the thunder growled into its own menacing being in the blacker from red cloud scudding sky, and the rain poured down in an instant deluge, steaming off the little ship.

The lightning struck once more, with its fast fifty prongs all separating, and discouraging helpers from the tenable cottages by literally burning paths for the due hell ball. Cooking a chimney and its failing rod, and putting scorched streaks on many walls and much land. The thunder gathered gloatingly, and the rain, that had been those drops of spilt blood for the wounded moment, thudded hissingly harder onto the ground, and all that was fragilely standing, or not quite.

It might have been no write-off crash. But the shuttle laid motionlessly in semi-interment. Nobody stirred inside.

And with the third lightning flash above still reprieved valley trees, the bolt began to mould in the incandescent womb.

At the Tavern, they didn't know about Edrak's plight. He hadn't contacted them on his way, wanting to surprise everybody. And not least, Soletra. All that they knew at the packing in building on the crest was the absolute nightmare again – of yet another storm back sooner than ever, placing everything even beyond the freakish. Men's faces were bleached white. Women shivered and often moaned in fright. Children clung in pitiful wailings to the skirts and tunics of those that could not allay them. A Lectan cat cringed and wauled in a cramped nook.

'Mercy on us!' said Rhada, as doors and windows automatically deployed their trebled defences the fellow was miserably losing more faith in. Illana started to the resonant clang of the resurrected metal shutters at the windows, then cowered beside her husband and simply prayed. As others prayed, overcrowding the bar room and looking more caught in a snare now than safe.

'Where's Soletra?' asked Rhada, when his friends' distraught daughters milled in his smitten sight. And as thunder pealed wall-shakingly louder, the gutters flooded this quickly, and there was that first demoniac scream, faintly yet on the back of the lightning going again for its hundred prongs before it had been shut off.

'I sent her to Edrak's mother. The poor soul won't leave her room,' the pale-lipped Illana replied on bigger starts and shivers.

'We're all poor souls,' muttered Rhada, and voiced what he felt had to be. 'The Moon Star is overdrawn with its luck. And one more storm like the last…'

'What in the world is happening to our part of the sector!' exclaimed popular patron, Hahn, wrestling nearer to the taverner in the affrighted throng. 'What in the very world!'

'Soletra, where are you off to?' Edrak's mother, the genteel and gentle Arella, asked with nervous surprise. 'I thought you were staying with me, child.'

'I won't be long. You'll be alright.' Soletra's patience was wearing threadbare, in that uncalm calm of hers, for the still beautiful, sorrel-haired woman, once like a second mother to her. This night, with the storm only here for her again that sooner she'd wished it with every fibre of her being, she could barely endure the kindly, affectionate creature clinging to her like the Inn vine, and as cloying as the bredala fruit.

'Soletra. Please.' Arella's tone was more loathsomely pleading to ears at knife-edge for any new sound between the thunder, and the rain, and the forming bolt.

'I won't be long,' Soletra more clippedly pronounced it, imperviously crossing to the door. Just outside it, she called, 'Anyway. Here is your friend Zea coming.' With her feet hurrying her on to the attic stairs up to her room, before anybody, and the fattish Zea puffing along, could apprehend her.

The girl locked the door of her roof room – out of bounds for her in any storm, never mind them now – and stood there, flushed and trembling, contemptuous for more defied rules, yet irresolute for a shaggy spell of her breath. She'd wanted to be where she was with a painful force. More twisting skewers of torment in her. Something had been so powerfully impelling her. Driving her relentlessly. But. She had arrived. And. What? She was only in another room, shuttered in triplicate. More of a steel cage for a madly fluttering bird. Yes. Just what?

In her quandary, thunder shook the room to its stressed joints. Rain beat as deafeningly on the roof, the chimney, and the doubtful conductor, and on the metal shutters, an angry, vengeful, torrential tattoo. The scream of the bolt sounded all at once closer – and closer, and closer – the new furies of every hell demon collecting in that scream.

Closer… and closer.

Soletra should have quaked with the room in abject terror, as everybody in the Tavern did, at the dreadful approach! And the luck of this place that could for sure be running out.

Instead… Instead, she was lunged head-on into wilder, rasher, madder churnings of excitement, going for broke, as abnormal and freakish as these storms, and then, swiftly and suddenly as any lightning strike, had that knowledge of what to do – and the incentive to do it that sheerly belonged to the lunacy, but had its own exorbitant, overriding compulsion.

Soletra didn't hesitate. Pressing the pertinent buttons in rafter shade, she had them open in a trice – the windows, and their protective shutters.

She had them open wide!

It just hurtled towards her – out of that tumultuous red-black night, but with the rain that could have petered for it. Coming at her – coming with its bloodcurdling scream at its pitch, and its crackling, sparking, blinding crimson electrical fires no rain could put out, anyhow…

The Zalan Bolt!

'That was near!' Rhada coldly sweated.

'As near as if it could have got inside!' Hahnn peakily said.

'If it had, we'd have known!' somebody else ditheringly said. 'And it's stopped its screaming. Must have burnt itself out.'

'It sounded too strong to have that quick a burn-off,' said a fourth person, grey about the gills.

'It can happen,' Rhada said croakily.

'Not often.'

'What is often and natural with this devilish glut of storms?' said Rhada on his kept croak.

'Perhaps Soletra and Arella, and others, would be safer down here,' Illana said, when her teeth weren't chattering as much.

'There is no safer these cursed days,' said Rhada, seeing little of that Moon Star luck left in the depository.

In the village below, the folk inhabiting – as yet – their loved homes, despaired of anybody being alive in the crashed shuttle that they couldn't get to. None of them. True, the bolt now seemed rampant at the top of the valley, giving a worrying and worried over-turn for friends and neighbours up at the Tavern. But they could never let that fool them. Any thunderous minute the flame ball could zag its extra terrifying trail back down there.

'The way these latest storms work, it's as though they're toying with us and the Moon Star,' somebody commented in the cottage closest to the crash site.

'If that wasn't medal-winning nonsense, or it was an any more cheering premise, I'd say you were right!' was a wincing reply, as beams could have been about to be jarred from their sockets in the calamitous thunder.

The shuttle still stayed motionless half in and out of the marshy furrows of ground. Except for its own jarrings from that seismic effect of the thunder. The rain again poured and steamed upon it, making the sludge more suckfully soft around it.

Soletra couldn't believe it.

Burningly blinded by the bolt, she had waited in her as swiftly and suddenly smashed esoteric excitement and its shower of kindling slivers, for the ring of fire to strike her.

It hadn't!

That awful, excruciating electrical heat on her face and body, as if to melt her flesh, drip it from the bones, and the awful, excruciating, eardrum-splitting screaming enough to implode her head, too, had just – just stopped! All of it scything sharply off!

And there had been nothing more there. Only the cooler rain spraying in.

She had fainted with shocked amazement. Sprawling her willowy length on the fast river of a floor before the gaping windows.

Now, on coming to, after however long she'd been insensible, she could only lay there – in the water, and more of it pattering on her, trying to be sure that she lived, groggily as it was. Could only lay there, with her scalded-feeling eyes shut in their constricted sockets, her stifled head a hotly hammered anvil, and her limbs limp and shivery as the vacated Jaal cocoon. Could only lay there – neither her old sweet self, or her more abhorrent new, but in a shock-invoked sort of hazed limbo between each.

She had just got the conviction she strove for in her heated and beaten mind's grasp, when she heard something above the storm, and her present state distancing it. Something somewhere in front of her, that now she couldn't believe she was hearing – even as she knew she shouldn't be hearing it. Or anybody.

She had to look up. Lift her turveying head, painfully prise open her eyes, and look up.

She was nearly blinded a second time! And as nearly shot a second time out of her senses to maybe never get back! By what she saw then.

She had thought she'd just seen the very worst thing you ever could.

She was having to think again!

And yet – yet – that climaxing lightning flash, and thunder crash later, where the too-many pronged lightning slashed the whole night asunder and soldered it there, and the magnitude of thunder shook the persevering Tavern like a rag doll, and dust from the stones, and when the repressed storm inside the girl suddenly burst the dam of her shocked limbo to rage forth in answer.

It was the very best thing. For her.

Downstairs, they could have sworn, in their frightened fancies, that the next bolt came with a positive wild, wanton triumph to its fury. As so it flamed back at the Inn, and circled it over and over again, and that close, telling of the baulking rod, you could hear the spherical fires charringly grazing the oscillating walls, and feel its withering heat blast through them. Then, when everybody was paralytically certain the rod would give altogether and that would be it, and were dying their thousand deaths, it brusquely flamed away valleywards on the saddle of the thunder, its screams getting fainter in the booms.

As soon as some shivering semblance of recovery was had for all, Rhada and friends, with a tearful, teetering Illana behind, raced cumbersomely upstairs to see how Soletra, Edrak's mother, and other women on that floor had fared.

Arella and company were alright, apart from being terrifiedly crushed together as Farren fish in their cans. But the room to where Soletra had reportedly flown – Zea had glimpsed her from the stairs – was locked and bolted, with only a cold stone silence inside it that frenetic calls and knockings ricocheted hollowly off. Rhada and the men had to resort to demolishing the door to get in, but whatever their natural fears, it was back to the unnatural with them – as it was more these days – at the scene beyond the negotiated timber shards.

The unshuttered windows yawned fully open, an unconditional invite for the bolt it had ignored for no reason known to mortals, as there wouldn't have been a room left, or a tavern, and the rain was sheeting in on everything in its tidy place.

But there was no Soletra.

It was all drenchedly desolate.

The storm was just about over when Edrak 'woke from the dead', too.

He thankfully still wasn't injured much. He may have passed out from that blow on his head when the ground had been met, with it fortunately like a wet sponge to only twist and dislodge metal and instruments, but all he had to show for the blow was a small, superficial gash on the temples, which had meanly bled. And as for his body, there was no more than the bruising and soreness, as if it had been on the paddles of the Harvester. The belt had also kept him firm in the modified impact. It had just been the inescapable bumps along the way.

It was the shuttle that was the write-off. Even for the softer landing. Badly bent, dented and breached, with smouldering inners. And sinking into the mud.

Edrak had no time to meditate upon his position. Or what had got him into it. The failing shields that should never have been. He had to abandon ship before he and the vessel were swallowed by the morass. He quickly fumbled to activate his undamaged transmitter wristband to send the emergency signal and his co-ordinates to Vaal High Speed Rescue – the baked controls would have preceded the shuttle's own signal on crash vector – and then he as fumblingly unbelted himself, and climbed more sorely towards the buckled door, which would have to be operated manually.

It took him strenuous, gruelling moments to get there, and more strenuous, gruelling moments to tug the door open, as it was sticking, becoming bogged in with the higher-sucking mud. He managed it. With strength of will more than that of his black and blue body, and the picture of his beloved Soletra like an exhorting angel in his mind; for him, the angel as yet unfallen. Panting hoarsely, he scrambled clumsily out and onto slanting, gouged metal above the soggy mud mouth. Tottering on the shuttle's wet, slippery roof, he could get his breath, mixed with a cough, feel the cold dark tell on his heated face, with stings of colder, thinning rain, rightly appreciate the drainings of lightningless thunder, and gear himself for the further exacting struggle of a more treacherously slippery, and not unsteep, climb onto doused, but even, ground.

The climb was as toilsome as anything, with one slow, sliding step up, a faster two back down, and it wasn't pleasant, for the squelch and gurgle of viscid suction close behind him, and taking the Star Racer deeper. But again, he managed it. As wet and mudded as the acclivity he'd made. Balancing now on sludge that wasn't quicksand. And grimacing to no more door in the shuttle.

Edrak started towards the sketchy outline of that nearest cottage, his tired, achy legs having to wade through intervening water puddling into the mud. The cottage must have been shuttered yet, masking any lights. But when the youth had tramped several more yards, he discerned to his dismay that the roof and chimney of the building had caved in. It was only the walls that were precariously standing, with no lights inside them any more – just heaps of slate and stone, and no sound from the people he'd known, and who'd worried about him, tragically buried underneath.

He slithered to a halt, his heartsick groan on the morbid silence, but for the grinding creak of the enfeebled walls.

He didn't move again, to his shins in a pond, until he heard weeping, lamenting voices being disjointedly disgorged from the saturated deeper throat of the night. He then tramped achily on in more hope, but with a no less hurting heart, in the direction of the sounds, seeing glimmers of light sprout somewhere in the ink wells ahead.

When he saw them in the closer bobbing storm lantern light, the scattered groups of gaunt men, moaning women, and clinging children, all as white spectres in the similar pallid glows, Edrak also saw the fate of Kratana now.

No habitation was left. There were only smoking ruins and rubble, or dissolved cinders like the old mill, and a wet black dust shroud for the many dead.

The destruction couldn't have been greater.

Edrak then didn't dare to think of the condition of the Inn above, and what could be with his dear ones, and more good people. He put his bruised head bleakly in his shaking, muddy hands.

Chapter 10

'A STORM THAT THINKS?'

The rescue shuttle from the Institute was there in record time. It would be if Edrak's wrist relayer had got its signal through alright. As it had. Just. The speed the purer extract of Linium fuel enabled these specific vessels to fly from sector to sector in minutes. With its soft, powerful whirring, and its neon emergency lights flitting alternate blue and amber over the area and the devastation, the circular, compact ship, that could land on Rault coin and any surface, did so only yards from Edrak. The door was open before it had settled itself on its stable hover inches from the boggy ground; its visible waves of suspension, acting tonight for the talonish struts, the shiftive, faint yellow annan rays crinkling smoked mud and pools.

Krael – a member of the rescue team – hastily disembarked, with Sanskril, of all persons, behind him, replacing any other members. Their anxiety for the youth, and their horror for the fallen village, was graven into the tight wax of their neon-reflecting faces. They half ran towards Edrak, as he stumbled physically and vocally towards them in his distress for Kratana, and fresh agonising fears for the Tavern aloft.

Sanskril, after his student's injuries were logged as minor, could at least comfort Edrak by assuring him the Moon Star looked miraculously unassailed yet again, but for more scorch marks, prospering on its crest to take in the rest of the refugees from the vale. It was just their communications that were out. Not even proffering static.

'We flew low over the place to be certain.' Krael endorsed this never expected news, unscrewing the flask of Zalan brandy for the overwrought Edrak to drink. He gave his friend a goodly measure, and next got the healing patch from the medical kit, for so blessed an exiguous injury for a head-on crash, be it in a quagmire. Sharp jutting instruments can still be killers!

'I must go up to the Inn,' Edrak spluttered, his emotional words colliding with an absent gulp of the warm, pungent brandy.

'No, Edrak. Time is of the essence,' Sanskril said urgently. 'Seeing all that has happened here, I've decided we're not waiting for dawn to move the machine. We're doing it tonight! It cannot be soon enough. The storms in your corner of the sector are beyond anything, abnormality itself, with their frequency and destructiveness. We must be quite ready for another one I can just about feel, which could wipe you out. And I am in earnest need of my trusted colleagues and work-force, including you, my most valued apprentice.'

'But, Sir! My mother, and Soletra, and—'

'I know, my boy, I know.' Sanskril undertoned his firmness of an order with sympathy. 'Only with the Tavern remaining staunchly standing, signifying no harm to anybody there, you can now best give service to those dear to you by devoting your strengths and efforts into helping solidify the hope you couldn't get to tell them of.'

Edrak had to acknowledge the truth of that. But it didn't

allay him, or make it any easier. He groaned again as he pushed the brandy aside.

'What I will do,' said Sanskril, patting Edrak's stoopier shoulder of tortured division, 'is leave Krael to assist and organise yonder sorrowful survivors, and take them up to the Moon Star. And he can stay there while the big aid shuttles we have notified have arrived, and report to us via their communications as to how everything is with your loved ones.'

Edrak nodded numbly, as he was torn more in two.

'Which says I'm expendable!' Krael declared with grim humour. But he was then himself encouragingly clasping Edrak's shoulder, and devoutly pledging, 'I'll get a message to you about affairs at the Moon Star as quick as I possibly can. But don't be afraid, Edrak. All will be well with yours. I'm sure of it.'

Edrak glanced at him with quiet gratitude and desperation.

'Come on, Edrak. You'll be better when you are doing something constructive,' said Sanskril wisely, the Professor not that long in judging an abler youth, and briskly, but kindly, ushering him to the shuttle, with the blinking amber and blue lights of the vessel blurring on Edrak's eyes. Edrak blinked himself, and didn't see plainer until he was strapped in the seat beside the scientist, adept at the controls. Everybody had a pilot's licence at Vaal, and the shuttle was swiftly hovering out of its suspension and upwards for swifter horizontal flight.

Sanskril went over the Moon Star again, to let Edrak have ungainsayable proof of the building astonishingly in one defiant piece. The shutters had been opened now, too, divulging healthy lights and healthier movements flicking across them. Edrak's spirits did lift in flutters – he could never guess, like his companion, at the new horror behind that activity. But he was still sawn apart when they were leaving the place on the far side of their fumeless exhaust.

He didn't speak until they'd cleared the wet, burnt borders of the ill-fated valley, and his own home ashes more immaterial, with his mother being safe. Then he supplicated his eminent master with all his baffled consternation.

'Sir, what is going on? What in the sake of pity, that seems to have deserted us here? Why are the storms hitting us, and only us? And as often as this. And so ferociously. With even the lightning before its formed bolt, that can go through shuttle shields at a first strike. I just cannot get my brain round it!'

'Currently, I cannot either,' Sanskril admitted. 'There is no recent detectable structural or gravitational imbalance exclusive to your region to in any way account for it. I repeat, I have spared Dralt and Toa to start that in-depth investigation, while I and others have got the machine into action, and with indeed every speed now. After tonight.'

'But it is such a fearful puzzle,' Edrak insisted. 'There has been nothing like it in the history of Zalan. It's almost as if…'

'Yes, Edrak?'

'It's ludicrous. But it's almost as if the storms are suddenly hosting an intelligence with a principal grudge against – us alone.'

When Sanskril didn't reply to that, Edrak said with a wriggle of embarrassment, 'I'm sorry, Sir. That was really preposterous! I trust you won't regard me the less for it.'

'On the contrary, lad,' Sanskril said then. 'Were it at all possible, it could be more of an explanation than anything. I'm only glad it isn't possible. A storm that "thinks" and could use the bolt like a prime weapon… It would pose the very worst peril for our planet. And as worse a peril to be found in the whole known universe.'

Edrak felt his warm embarrassment go cold to his bones at his mentor's words, and only blessed in that coldness, the ludicrousness.

Everything was discomforting enough. To just Professor Quent's hypothesis having inveigled in more about the bolt and regeneration.

Chapter 11

'THE VALADRIAN
IS GOING TO WAR.'

Pilot and passenger were each silent after that. Silent and pale in the blue and amber of the emergency lights Sanskril had kept on for an unhindered run to the Institute.

They only spoke again when they were seeing a floodlit Vaal turreting up with the twin peaks to these unmolested, starry skies, and then beneath their craft the shuttle rail beginning to switch on its own floodlights.

'Anyhow, we can assemble daylight for the transportation,' said Sanskril, swerving smoothly left for the Institute.

'It was kind of you to come for me yourself, Sir,' Edrak thought to say, as on their bird swoop approach he spotted industry with a mile long I in key locations. It was especially a seethe of motion in the central courtyard, where the vast, girder-enclosed descender pad, with its sufficient size and strengths of Zalan steel, was capable of taking any object whatsoever. Beside it, and ready to be loaded onto it, was Sanskril's invention never the more relied upon, and its compressly-packaged paraphernalia, all securely covered in sheets of everything-proof metallic cloth, and still looking as off-the-scale bizarre. When brought aboard the pad, the unmoderated monstrosities – also packaged in more new hope for Edrak – would be carried carefully down the deep shaft inside the rocky escarpment, and onto the moving road at the bottom, winding out to Vaal's private rail track joining with the main departure route for land transferable goods. Stout and skilled men, who were to do the loading and shaft ride, were excitedly and loyally waiting by the machine; cleverer others stood farther about in groups to confer, watch, and follow. And then there were all the batches of tenser shufflers on the outskirts of the courtyard, who wouldn't be going, but wanted their protruding eyeful while they could.

'That I could be spared for,' said Sanskril. It could have been Edrak's eagerer observing age since his gratified remark, and as green lights started to flash above the steel lift and one side of the girder work slid away. 'My skills weren't required for the packing up, and that being so lengthy a task, I had ample time to come in hopeful person to make sure my best student was intact.' The last with a levity to belie the scientist's anxieties, having been as grave as Krael's for that asset of a young man on every count.

'Thank you, Sir,' the more moved Edrak said, a trifle gruffly.

'Which, to be praised, you are.' Sanskril might not have heard him. 'I need you intact on this night!'

It was all accomplished in half the estimated time. Due to scientists, apprentices, and labourers alike continuing sedulously at their stations. Only a couple of hours after Edrak and Sanskril had arrived back at Vaal to oversee the tricky loading of the machine onto the Descender, the great, super smooth, blue steel shuttle train, with its special closed-in wagons, was starting to move. Was starting to thrum slowly and cautiously down the line, with the magnetised double wheels easing into that rhythmic, refrainic clicking, seeming to say to all attuned ears tonight, 'The Valadrian is going to war… The Valadrian is going to war…'

It was something of a spectacle itself. The floodlit rail track changing night into brightest day. The tremendous train, with its first largest, loftiest, extra reinforced wagon, more like an outsize steel container, and then the two large, not as high but longer, wagons placed well apart. The revered Institute emblem luminously on each blue side. The lights on the rod-bearing engine and on all the bevelled carriage roofs, which at short intervals flashed green and purple, snappy spurts of rich colour in the artificial day, which proclaimed the awe-inspiring cargo and right of way.

It was a sight never to be forgotten. Whatever the outcome.

Professor Sanskril, of course, travelled inside that first wagon the machine was entrusted to, with his other top-ranking colleagues. He was guarding his brainchild as a mother would her newborn. Edrak was in the second wagon with his fellow apprentices; in their charge the coils of miles-running cabling, and multifarious fitments. The choice labourers occupied the third wagon, with a dismantled, portable steel lift about filling the carriage, for getting the machine up Dallan-Torrin.

Edrak's companions excitedly chattered fifty to the dozen. But the youth himself was understandably quieter, sharing his excitement with worry for those at the far-off Moon Star he was still unenlightened about. Communications with the tavern had remained out when he'd left Vaal. And neither yet had he heard from Krael on his personal transmitter, though that could be because his friend had been delayed in the valley, up to his neck in the no mini-feat of dealing on his own with suffering survivors.

Edrak could just pin on hearing from Krael at the first likely chance. Maybe before the train klaxon next sounded for the Eddon snake bend and tunnel, marking halfway to the border.

Chapter 12

ANOTHER NIGHTMARE
AT THE INN...

As it was, things were even harder for Krael than Edrak had assumed. The student of agriculture, who'd always opted for amalgamating the seat of learning with all the fun of the fair, was undergoing the most trying and heart-sickening work of his thus unready young life. For the pathetic straggle of survivors that had made their own trialsome way to the Tavern, there were many others, widely dispersed in the weeping frenzy or dazed despair for the loss of families and homes, and Krael was having to singlehandedly help, comfort, and organise to get them up the valley, while the aid shuttles were coming. And then, somewhere in his numbly noble endeavours, an orphaned girl – with yellow hair curling to its wetness and big, helpless, yellow-flecked bluest eyes, as pretty as a sun sylph of Via – had attached herself to him, and attached was it! She was hanging hamperingly onto his every move. Not that Krael was complaining there.

But at worn and torn last, he somehow succeeded in manoeuvring all the good people he sorrowed for in their straits into one heartbreaking cluster of mourning, and shepherding them aloft on a soddenly blackened path. With that aid

95

from the townlands appearing in powerful purrings, intermittent klaxons, and dark splitting neons, to say he'd really done it quicker than he'd thought, or would have thought to. The first sizeable shuttle landed, the struts employable here for the raised stone cruiser pad, when he was staggering squishingly with the forlorn folk across the sludgy tavern yard, not neglecting the girl limpet on his exerted arm.

Only the nightmare wasn't over on him guiding his poor, snivelling flock into the heat-blackened, but so indomitably standing, Moon Star. Another nightmare just waited to distend it, at Krael being met with more fear, anguish, and confusion from Rhada, and all the able-bodied gone, and the rest, and Illana and the women, wringing hands with hearts, as they paced or bunched together. To whom yet more tearful valley refugees were no antidote; the inn straining at the seams with misery.

Krael, when he could coax his lovely hanger-on into getting attended to in exchange for his pledge to return to her, soon got to know what was amiss. Which sank his heart lower, to his slushy boots, for Edrak.

'Soletra has vanished in the midst of the storm! But how can this be?' He stared incredulously at Tyn, the lame man who'd haltingly told him this.

'We don't know how it can be!' The man shook a nonplussed head. 'It was just an empty room, and open windows, could you believe!'

Krael couldn't that either.

'She weren't hit by the bolt. There's always something left – be it only a ladleful of ashes,' the older man, Nethar, said more macabrely, away from Illana's demented ear.

'They could be finding – something. As we speak,' commiserated Tyn.

'But, how could Soletra get out? Why should she get out!' Krael horrifiedly wondered.

'Questions don't have answers these days, young sir,' said Tyn. 'And, no more do we know all the questions.'

'It's not like Loriste's disappearance,' said the grislier Nethar. 'It was after the storm with her. And she was seen going off. On the heels of that dark one. And no more can we blame that stranger tonight. He plainly went around that affair, and could by now be at the other side of the planet, or not any longer on it.'

'No. We can't blame him tonight – Zaltar Valada,' said Tyn, nervily stopping short on realising the unmentionable name had passed his lips, in this time become as black as Krella's pit.

'Is – that what they call him?' said Krael, with a slight start.

The reply was a silent, self-reproachful nod from Tyn, as Nethar warded off the evil eye.

'Are you sure?'

'We're not likely to forget what was never spoken among us, but carved in the black of a curse on our minds,' Tyn said, not much over a gratery whisper.

'Edrak certainly never spoke it,' Krael murmured more mechanically.

'He wouldn't, if he couldn't hear it from us. The fellow was just the described weird wanderer from out of the storm for him.'

'But what is it, lad? You're looking a bit odd,' said Nethar, with a narrower glance at Krael.

'That's right,' agreed Tyn, with his sharper squint at the

youth.

'It's that name. It seems sort of familiar,' said Krael, rumpling his night-taxed brow more to that chord having been distinctly plucked.

'You mean, you could have heard it before!' exclaimed Tyn, in stark surprise.

'It's more like I've read it – somewhere. But not, I think, as the name of a man,' Krael said slowly and studiously.

'Which it isn't,' shivered old Nethar. 'I can think it's more fit for a devil of darkness from the mythical, malformed world – T'hhaldaria.'

'I must try to remember about this,' Krael said, mostly to himself, and then he was as slowly and studiously turning to walk off. 'I feel it could be… important.'

The two men gazed after him, as puzzled and uneasy from this.

Krael had to go outside, where he could breathe his deepest since the fairground ride had braked, and clear his overburdened brain.

And yet, why did he sense it was important? the memory tug, he had to ask in his browner study yards from the swollen inn of wretchedness, and in the damp air like it detained raindrops still on his frowning face. With him receiving the only available answer – he just did, to a dismal rustle of Xylax leaves above him, and a splintered cobble crushing under his feet, heavy from his heart being in them.

In fact, it fast growingly felt that important, it clouded everything else. With the added unenviable dilemma of a transmission he should make, and couldn't.

Chapter 13

THE SLIPPER ON TARRA MYYA

The time passed quickly, for all the careful slowness of the rail shuttle. Excitement for everybody, with those worries on the heart side for an Edrak more than ever so unsuspecting for them, had raced the Zalan clock ticks by.

Edrak felt they'd only been minutes on the wooded straights and curves, with their smatterings of verdure tunnels and mirror rock, water-reflecting viaducts, when the klaxon sounded differently, lower, and more courteously, for the borders being crossed into his own sector. Its next sounding, on a now discernably ladened, unrestful atmosphere, would be for the sighting of a dark plateau, soon to be floodlit, too.

'Moment of truth coming,' said Shan, a gangly fellow apprentice.

Which hushed the talkativeness, and made Edrak still quieter in his sensitive perceptions of home and storm ground.

It was loyal patron Hahn who found the first one further on the westerly way. The tiny slipper was wetly upside down on a rocky declivity.

Rhada snatched it from him with an agonised cry, 'My

Soletra's! My girl's!'

'Courage, my friend,' said Hahn, his storm lamp, that daylighted yards, bleaching all the fear-etched faces in this band of searchers, of the many of them that had plumped for trying westwards, not as much prolifically inland. 'The shoe is soaked but unmarked, and proves we are in the right direction, when the rain has washed out all trails.'

Rhada wasn't listening. He bulkily lurched himself into getting to the bottom of the slope, shouting huskily and anguishedly, 'Soletra! Soletra!' With his voice and its echoes stranded on a remorseless silence.

'It's not good, though,' muttered Le'at, another of the motley, but estimable, group that flexed to follow the taverner.

'Who says it's good?' Hahn soberly responded. 'And we're going into tricky terrain. How on earth, too, could the girl have got as far as this – never mind why?'

'This is like poor Loriste,' said Vren, the youngest searcher there.

The other slipper was found a copse-strawed, slopier distance later.

It was beside a ferny hollow on Tarra Myya. That three-mile, stranger tract, where the oldest, oddest trees grew, and the tallest, oddest plants, and the ground, wavy as water, could be stony, with abiding rain pools, or shaggily rugged with bluey-green grass sighing with and without the whimsical western wind. This slipper was as wet, but not unmarked. There was a smear of black slime over the dainty heel that didn't accord with the ochre tract mud, and that the pitifully crouching Rhada mumbled something unintelligible to in his distress, and knocked off at once. The slime plopped with a curious audibility, for what it was, onto a fallen broad, flat 'plate plant' leaf, and spread all over the blue striped green as more of it than it had looked, forming like another skin that stretched in ugly black shimmers.

Hahn was the only one of the other men to see the repulsive 'plop', and 'blackly fleshed' leaf, as he was nearest Rhada, with his bracing hand on the taverner's hunching shoulder. He'd never encountered slime like that before, and yet – it sort-of reminded him about something…

'How much farther can Soletra have got! And barefoot now!' Le'at morbidly wondered, standing with the others by an age-crippled tree. 'We'll shortly be at the Torrin Plateau!'

'That we will!' somebody else said.

'We have to find her soon.' Hahn exigently elbowed the singular slime aside, and helped the distressed Rhada up, with the two slippers hugged to his chest. But the sturdy, grizzled fellow still had to glance back before the quitting of the spot, at a shiny black leaf, and a more irksome sense of reminiscence.

'Yes. We must find her soon,' said young Vren– always a discreet admirer of Soletra – as they all trekked through Tarra Grove, with these trees, older than the hills, stooping and drooping over them, and dankly dripping more stored raindrops on them.

But another rougher, grassier mile on was as unproductive as ever.

'This is only more of what is beyond all knowledge and reason!' somebody baffledly said to a chorus of restive assent from everybody but Rhada, who dropped a slipper in his stricken stumble, and Hahn, who bent to retrieve it.

It was the second slipper, from the Tarra tract. Hahn joggedly saw what Rhada obviously hadn't, for his distraction and having had the dear footware in his knifed heart's hug. That the faint slime stain on the fabric was somehow now as black as the defilement had been, but more crozzled-looking where that had been unctuously smooth, and that it wasn't quite the shape of a stain any longer, only rather as if red-hot things had slithered over the heel. As well as which, when Hahn leaned lower for a closer scrutiny of the slipper, there was the definite whiff of a scorched smell from it…

Rhada was about to do his slipper snatch again, but hesitated on seeing it for himself, the grotesquely graduated stain.

Then he said, with more clarity than he'd had for a while, but also more fear and grief, becoming undone in both, 'I know what did that – if I tried not to! I know what it is! Where it is from – shed like the Hedlar does a scale. I touched – all of it! That night! I was the only one who did! By the stars of Ranomath, the only one! So, I have to know!'

And, though others sadly thought that the taverner's distress was starting to unhinge his mind, Hahn, even before the dark dawning, could only wish there was no more to it than that…

Chapter 14

THE YALSKRID TEXT

Round about that time, Krael was having a dawning, too, in the Moon Star yard. It came all at once. Lightning-prong style.

'I have to get back to the Institute!' he said. And didn't fritter another second.

With his Vaal credentials and clean pilot's licence, he had no hassle in commandeering the smallest inactive aid shuttle, promising to return it as soon as he could. He also remembered that other promise he was gladder to keep. He hurried back to Faretta, the 'sun sylph' girl, who was weepily awaiting him, with her cuts and abrasions eased and healing but not her heart of loss. He suggested she accompanied him. Not to Vaal, but he could leave her on the way at his parents' ultra-modern residence by the luminous lake, where she would be lavishly cared for until he could see her again.

'I understand you might not want to go to my sector,' he concernedly began.

But she whispered interposingly with her tears, and her hand needily grasping at his, 'Please! Do take me! There is nothing for me here now.'

Krael, sorry for her as he was, felt a leap of joy inside him that was a beam of beacon light to him in this darkest night.

He at last might have met his own loveliest sweetheart, and she was safer than Edrak's Soletra, whatever had befallen the poor girl…

He had witness of Faretta gratefully ensconced and lovingly treated at his fashionable but homely abode, and re-boarded the shuttle to steer right of the lucent lake and paddling silver trees, for the Institute.

His tiny transmitter lay on the seat beside him, haunting him with that call he was gearing himself to make before sighting the Twin Mountains. The lie he had to tell so that Edrak wouldn't be deviated from his part in that all vital work, until prayed-for better news to be, that would bring Krael absolution.

The corridors to his eastside Department of Agriculture and Ecology, as the other corridors to them, were more desolate than the ghostly Ghothall Canyons. It wasn't the lateness; and anyhow, Vaal people were about at all hours. But everybody, and that was everybody with 'droid stand-ins', would be on Sanskril's turf tonight. Spectators of the monitoring of the Valadrian's journey and then, hopefully, of the historic events it would unfold at its destination.

Krael didn't loiter in the expansive upper rooms of the stockier east tower, with their own substitutive, impersonal robotica and automatism. He just got the electronic key from the box on Professor Krrosan's not tidiest of desks, and went swiftly down the steel spiral staircase, that low lit itself at a tread, right to the cryptish bowels of the tower. He shouldn't be doing any of this, he knew. Not without permission. But needs, however vague, must.

Krrosan, the most eccentric professor at the Institute and the one Krael was helping with his history hobby, had taken over the bottom chamber – only occasionally used to store surplus stuff – for his dabblings into the mysteries and wonders of Zalan's Ages. The man with pepper-coloured hair, beard, and beetling brows, liked to keep his research into the past separate from his work of the future, and found the isolation and atmosphere of the cellar more inspirational for the former. Whenever he could, he retreated here, with nobody to disturb him or pry. Not that they would. With that hair hue, Krrosan could be a tartar of the first water.

Krael opened the octangular door and stepped into another light coming on that should have been much brighter, but wasn't tonight; some filaments could be on the blink. The cellar was always a place that was a tad spooky. An octangular room as well, of many corners, that squatted under a pressing vaulted roof, lugged up by leanified pillars, it was more like a sepulchre to the youth, and as dusty, with as stale and musty an odour. Krrosan studied, not spring-cleaned. But tonight, it was spookier than ever, with the dimmer light lending a hand. With a hush you could hear loud, for the more silent eve of the rest of the tower, uncannier shadows slunk in all those nooks and crevices and over the arched edges of the roof. Stacks of cobwebby crates here and there had the look of hiding what unimaginables could be waiting to pounce out. Then you had Krrosan's makeshift desk in the exaggerated depths, that was the punish dead-ringer for a bier, with none of the proverbial mess of books and parchments on it, detracting from it.

Chiding himself for silly fancy that was never his forte, Krael strode the stouter over the bare, veined, stone floor towards the deceptive desk, not as deceptive on him reaching it, and its plainer Krrosanian state. What he was after wouldn't be in that desktop disorder. Repeating his apologies to the absent professor, he switched on the desk lamp really required in this dimness, but was there for its other advantages for the tasked eye, and started to rifle through the contents of the hulking drawers in their varied old sour stages. Krael never cared for old aromas!

It was in the third drawer. Aslant in its protective Oltskin folder, as it was submerging beneath yellowy-brown, rolled or flattened parchments.

It had been acquired by Krrosan eight months ago, on his annual vacational expedition to the fusty hubs of inner city museums, galleries, and curio shops. It was a copy of an exceedingly ancient scroll, that was all rifts and wrinkles and fragilely going to driest decay, on which a rough, shoddily learned hand of those far bygone days had written some kind of text in one of Zalan's earliest languages, Yalskrid. A language that had been obsolete for more years than the Dallan-Torrin bird, and was only of any consequence now to the odd historian, serious or sideline, or the archaeologist unearthing unseldom artefacts from its era.

The professor had told Krael, to whom he'd showed the copy three months since, when the lad had been assigned as his 'honoured' helper, that the original scroll – as portrayed – had indeed gone to intimated decay in the Middle Age, leaving this only known copy to date, with the added value of it being as anonymously tooled as the original, and having the weight of years behind it itself. In the matter of how old it was, the over every sun and moon, Krrosan had cause from experts to put it at two centuries, and had explained to Krael, the very interested party in his coup with an inquiring youthful mind to be fostered, the reason of its excellent condition that could dispute its longevity. The professor had said that, unlike the archetype made of primitively pressed J'dala plant leaves, not as enduring as the J'dala sap-ink for the wording, the emulative document had been done in the same ink but on a light, elasticated paper that was as imperishable, patented in the later period, and shaping the paper of now. And, as well as that, the transcript had permanently been kept in the foolproof folder purchased with it.

Krrosan was also an enthusiast for languages, and particularly Yalskrid – the hardest tongue to master on or off planet, which was still another bonus here for him. In the joys of challenge he flourished on, when he preferred to decipher anything by the old methods of long, trialsome cogitation, plain graft, not the new high speed translation techniques, that to Krael would have been a boon.

The professor had begun the 'graft' too. But he'd had to grudgingly stop when everything else had stockpiled, and wouldn't be getting back to it for a while. He hadn't let on to the privileged Krael what he'd translated up to then, saying he would have to wait until he'd finished all the text. He'd just given him an appetiser, telling him it appeared to be an account of some legend, of sorts, from when Zalan's time was new born. Krael tentatively took the copy from the folder and, so as not to overhandle it, laid it like a raft on the sea of the other miscellaneous material mayhemly awash on the desk. He used the handiest desk lamp benefit by initiating magnification beam, and gazed closer at the durable page, with its script in crabbed clumps to represent paragraphs:

Evolving from Zalan's first form of alphabet, Yalskrid was

the queerest written, as much as spoken, language you could wish to see, whatever it read on this page. The lettering was cramped and hunching, scrawly at the top but club-footed, and sloped in many directions. And if that wasn't enough, there were the just as cryptical mini-symbols to divide the words, and blotchy asterisks to thrice underline, pronunciate, or end a protracted sentence. It was all a real maze, and a lot for the cleverest brain. However, three-quarters of the way down this illustrative page, there were those two words that were surprisingly more legible, if previously no more understandable, in the ungainly script. They were larger, clearer, not as ravelled, without the interjecting symbol or asterisk, only a thicker underlining. Like they'd been penned with a slower, deliberate precision – maybe from more reverence? Or graver misgiving?

Krael recalled how the words had strongly impressed upon him that day. And not just for being clearer than the rest of the scrawl, but mostly for the something about them that had curiously, and much short of pleasantly, compelled and held him, and echoed unwantedly in his head. He had forgotten them afterwards when the text was out of his sight, and Krrosan was running him ragged between his own mountain of work. Or he'd thought he had. Evidently, it was only on the surface he'd forgotten. His subconscious mind hadn't. That must have stayed impressed by the two 'pre-eminent' words, letting them lurk low there until tonight, when a frightened Kratana man had spoken them…

'Zaltar Valada.'

And now Krael felt more than re-impressed.

He had no foggiest idea in the length and breadth of the known universe. What it could mean. A stranger of today, from another world and another galaxy, wherever they could be, with a name devised from letters of Yalskrid – a long defunct language from deep in the nebulous mists of their planet Zalan's past.

He could never have any idea.

But he felt ice-tipped barbs of a fresh kind of fear entirely, digging into him, flesh, marrow and bone, and turning him like frosting earth. The kind of fear that had no description and nothing to call it by. That couldn't ever be ignored and pushed aside. Such as had been testified to at the Moon Star, to do with all those who had seen the sinister traveller.

Although this did engender the instinctive knowledge of his next move. He unsteadily rifled some more through that drawer. It obliged him again. Wedged in the Yalskrid Manual for the grafters refusing to cheat on their mental prowess, as Krrosan had pompously put it, was the Professor's translation so far of the text. It was only the scratchily-scribbled draft yet on the well-thumbed jotter page, the scribble nearly its own spindly answer to Yalskrid, with corrections and crossings out in purple to jumble it up more.

Krael as gingerly positioned the translation beside the transcript, two counterpoising muddles.

But Krrosan had made more than a start, Krael deduced. With ancient and modern sentences, and paragraphs meticulously aligned, he'd got to about over half of the text, only give or take an inch from those two words. His mental prowess at a leap! The youth chose to switch to another notch with the lamp's inbuilt magnifier, and screwed up his eyes in his acutest concentration on Krrosan's compliant jotter squiggles.

Krael did alright – eventually – by anybody's standards.

There was the odd word or letter he could have erred with, but solving the bulk and piecing in the corrections, he definitely got the gist of the translation, and that much of the text – which went as follows – and was eerily enough for him.

It was thus spoken, when Zalan's time was young.

He rides in fury on the wings of the storm.

At an iller hour will he come in the skin of Jadarass, custodian of Euils, and of the crawlers of the dark, and their slurring slime broods, that will enable him to at last be as of two, on being only seen as one. Such that is but for a short while, and once every hundred years, or more, until the next wizadry of she who is found.

She of beauty, goodness, and innocence he will cruelly defile, and with her fiercely consuming love for him, which will blunt her fears of what he is, and how fatefully she will serve him.

She will give wholly of her life force to him, and with it the stronger for the new night of her soul. As snow white purity stained black has the greater potency, for it to be bindinely beaten on the anvile over infernal fires.

Woe to she that is taken
Woe to she that is not.
Woe to the dwellers of Zalan.

For he will now forever endure as the two. And will be all powerful. All terrible. A nether god, with nobody and nothing that can stop him.

Our planet shall fail, and with his gained freedom of the stars, other worlds shall fall to him too. And he even may ...

But that was the break-off point for Krrosan's other duties interfering, the Professor only hurrying in more squiggles of the condensed comment: 'Dawn of time fairy tale? Promoter of legend and superstition? The answer to such tendencies towards outdated beliefs in us – the Zalan nation?'

Krael stood stock still. As inanimate as the desk. His rounder stare was bolted and barred on that jotter page. The sweat coldly collected on his shivering flesh, with a clammy trickle of it down his ramrod spine.

He wasn't thinking of first legends and fairy tales, or from whence the superstitious nature of their race had sprung.

He was thinking of fantastic and frightening familiarities.

Of Kratana's lately stranger in the storm – said to be flagrantly unafraid, with his mysterious power, and mesmerising charm, and menace.

Of Loriste.

Of the then discovered other like affairs of disappearance and death two centuries ago – about the very age of the transcript.

And of Edrak's Soletra. In some way…

While, he didn't know what to think at all!

And as he stood on there, the main dimmer light and the brighter desk lamp began to flicker in quite disquieting turn and the lamp into dimness, too, with the nearest shadows becoming overly convincing simulations of hideous, half alive things sidling only the nearer to him. And after the biggest flickerings more bidders of the dark, Krael had the scalp and spine-creeping, blood-congealing feeling that somebody had just stepped into the room and was moving up closely behind him. Somebody that was something that should never be – and that should never be there… ever.

The feeling was that strong, with the nerve-gnawing warnings joining on, he didn't chastise himself for fancy then, and gave the shiver outright which galvanised him into action and swung him trepidly round.

He saw no more than the shadows he'd had his locked spine on, regrouping like an ebon vapour pall between him and the door. The door he had left open, hadn't he? But it was now shut, and grovelling into the deepening shade, as if it soon wouldn't be there. Yet for the fact that Krael saw nobody… nothing… he couldn't get rid of the feeling – he wasn't alone.

He wasn't alone at all.

The warnings were next for him to go! To shake the dust of this room off his feet! And he was heeding them!

He just made quailing time to write down on a page he ripped from the smaller desk jotter those two words he had to know the meaning of, and return not as tidily the transcript and translation to the drawer. Then, with no further ado, it was out with the flicking desk lamp and his championship sprint to the door. There was only the horrible thought, when he was at the door – that it wouldn't open. Another feeling, more than fancy, that could have taken devilishly from the Yalskrid text.

The door did open, his superfluous vigour with it, that could have sent him toppling again into the room of gross shadows and grosser illusions, and he was up the stairs five at once, rattling the rail.

No way was he ever going back there without anybody else!

And not with company for a fistful of months!

Chapter 15

AND ON DALLAN-TORRIN...

The plateau was as wide as quarter of a sector, and as high as a small mountain from the Aradas Range. It was treeless, with skimpy other vegetation withered away, and had nothing any more to declare there had ever been the horned, scaly Torrin bird, whose giant briar ground nests had infested its namesake tableland that long, long ago. There could honestly be no righter location for the Valadrian. Width and height exact. No clearing to do. And the flattest yardage to be wished for on the northern edge, along with practically the straightest cliff face.

Sanskril was over suns and moons himself for the rightness, with Edrak and all orbiting after him. Edrak, that would have had honed anxieties chaffing at his excitements, if he hadn't on arrival got the brief teletext from Krael, obviously up to his elbows yet in aid relief, saying, 'Your loved ones okay. Be in proper contact later.' That atrocious lie that had to dress as the necessary truth.

The ideal situation, and the increased exigence, primed this work as well. Lubricated these wheels. There were no problems or obstructions here either. Only, could it be, even more assiduity and efficiency in thrill, and taller-propped hope tighter lacing close, comradely harmony.

The lift was put together at 'mach speed' by the labourers, and Sanskril's machine taken up on it to the top of the plateau, to be precisely and soundly placed on that flat-as-glass rock by the Professor and his select team, in their own one confluent motion of like speed, while the other components were being loaded and raised. The ablest of the labourers, apprentices in the offing, also helped the rest of the Professor's team, with Edrak among them in that finer unsuspecting fettle, in the prepping of the primary link of cabling for its attachment to the machine, and its magnetic descent of the suitable cliff face, to then be connected with the several thicker ground cables; these timed to self-lay and run to the main power line of the nearby Maradan Plant.

Only when the test of them all – this head-on meeting between the machine and the bolt – had been prayer-answeringly passed, would anything be permanentised. The machine, that was otherwise indestructible, with its integrating linear metal and Zalan steel – both ores together that could stave a rogue asteroid attack – would have the ridged bases of its tripod legs sunk deep into the Torrin surface rock, and riveted there by the Ranafren clamps that would ensure complete immobility, the sway before nothing. And the primary cabling would be bedded as deep in that cliff face with the Ranafren tools, and the ground cables sealed in on their own laid run, at the right depth there, to the K.11 Power Conduit.

When Sanskril's invention, and the miracle of engineering, had been erected on its appointed site, it looked more than ever like something bang out of a first-class fantasy, or the best Kratana fireside fable. A looming, weirdly, and wonderfully unreal structure glinting the strangely mergeful, moving blues and greens of that costliest amalgamation of metals. A futural enigma on a plain, ancient spot, with the floods that could be the lights of a thousand star cruisers hewing it from the cosmic black stone of the night.

It looked extra predominant, too… extra commanding… extra awesome… extra… everything, in that meaning-business mode.

A metal nemesis without doubt or question!

And more than ever, Edrak couldn't stop staring at the contrivance. His eyes and mind avidly re-absorbed through thrill the out-of-any-world design of it, with its unending complexities. The chunky-legged, wedge-footed, tripod-like part of the mechanical life form of Taraid 4, which was studded with tiny electro pods, and twined with conundrums of varifold wiring, coated in all proof Nadra, liquefied steel… The rectangular containment casket on top of the tripod, not melded to it, but 'growing' from the legs, that was covered with bigger electro pods, and more perplexities of broader, Natra'd wiring… On top of the casket, and again 'growing' from that, the huge, cowl-shaped contraption, the nucleus of the machine, which, slanting to the correct designated degrees like a lifting head, was made of a sturdy metal mesh, with the countless electros here mixed amongst a quantity of magnetic pulse points. And this complicated Natra'd wiring, wound as intricately many times through the web work metal, no less indestructible than the bulk.

How the Valadrian functioned could be simplified for the edification of the uninitiated. Or so Edrak had simplified it for Rhada and the others back home, who'd be wanting to know in hopefully victorious due course. The machine self-activated at the very first lightning fork, lighting up itself, and powering up the electrics and magnetics. The super-strength electromagnetic hood would draw the lightning at once, to hold it and divest it of, and ensnare, the first moulding bolt. The mesh trap would then neutralise the bolt, whatever its ratio of force in any remnants of lightning, and speedily transfer it to the ultimately safe bounds of the casket. And in the casket, the ring of fire would be as speedily converted into a tame and tractable energy, with none of its force impeded, that in turn would be transferred through the union of the attachment cabling and the ground lines to the Maradan Plant, ready to utilise this cornered, infinite energy for the good of all Zalan, instead of the bad.

Edrak soon had gaping company, with his fellow apprentices and the labourers longer in their own finishing-up tasks; then some of the Professors came along, leaving Sanskril to his final conferrings with his higher-ranking associates. And there they all stood, in a semi-circle of silent, awed adulation – worshippers at a metal shrine – until Sanskril had done, and also came along, with his choice group at his jauntier side, to briefly activate the machine now as the last check on that. It pleased him to operate it manually, as he had in the earlier days. The remote control from the later successes would be for tonight, that last test on the field, before the machine's automatic programming could be engaged from then on. And it pleased everybody else to witness the Professor do it manually. It was a gesture of more moment 'on the field'. More fitting for the crux. The qualifying hand of Zalan's favourite son perhaps, to be on the spearhead lever.

The whole device lunged into life in that way to still startle the observers. It loudly hummed and drummed with all that steady, titanic power, and every square inch of the metal lit vividly up, hyper-fluorescent blues and greens that sparked to a livelier motion of changing and interchanging, with the clashing contrast of the myriads of electros flaring and sparking more, in hyper-fluorescent orange and amber.

And so switched on, in its entirety and its habitat, the Valadrian could claim its niche in the halls of the fearsome, along with the lightning and its fire child it was to be pitted against. All as hotly and dazzlingly radiant, to a medium of pain, as the terribly multiplied prongs and savager wheel of flame. And with the sound of it, that metal heart strumming mightily on the supercharged voltage strings, which had to be as threatening as the consort thunder.

'More of a sight you don't see every day,' somebody murmured.

Another person said, 'It's scarier, too!'

And another, 'Something like that… just has to work!' A ripe chorus of overawed comments ensuing and intermingling, a river of many rushing notes, as Sanskril next put Remote Control through its paces.

Edrak just let his patience excitedly thin to watch the hopes of Zalan go into that 'deadly serious action'. And with the most fillip yet for his faith, he could permit himself to picture it – the drawn lightning firing and crackling its live crimson forks into the sparkingly answering blue-green and amber brilliance of the cowl, and kept there for the bolt to be caught in its fiery birth… screaming awfully then at being trapped.

Krael was glad to be back in his hi-tech faculty. Where the pleasanter future, as opposed to the darker past in which he'd stepped, was defined by the light and the bright and the spanking new. But unease was coldly and clammily clawing at him still. He no longer felt… anybody… anything that shouldn't be, behind him. But, of something he wasn't free. He was, if nothing else, tied with cords still dark to an ancient text – and a man called Zaltar Valada.

There was no return ticket yet for his merry-go-round. He couldn't even see the vendor there any more.

Edrak's iller-learning friend, with the tutor of fear now over the one of sorrow, got to where he wanted to be with that jotter page like ice in his tremulous fingers, and hastened towards the main computer swelling its chest of flash modernity and top classifications. He sat at it, with his unease of the bemusing moment replacing his usual airy confidence in his expertise, and twitchily clicked on and straight to the Archive Files of the Language Translation Programme. At the enquiry sign, he typed in 'Yalskrid', and with a more bungling touch than would have miffed a babe in arms! Another prompt sign, this going on and off, bade him to proceed. He took a breath that could have cracked with tension. That did.

He typed in just those two words he felt were the dark key to it all, the dark core of the age-old text, careful amidst his 'bunglingness' to keep the accuracy of the spelling, and then he waited…

Only seconds later, tapped suspensefully away by his iced fingers on the desk, the computer superiorily gave him what he required.

And yet, by all the millenniums of Zalan and the lives of

man – he didn't!

Krael recoiled out of his chair.

The white-faced young man, with a title for his fears, and his mind and spirit in a tailspin, traded the aid shuttle for a faster Vaal model, and was off, with no more ado, the Institute towers being smoked by his craft's exhaust when he remissly flooded the tubes.

Sanskril switched off the machine and ordered the de-mesmerised team to leave the plateau and make for the shelter of the train that was the safest as any, waiting on the mile away track at Kaladan crossing.

'A storm has to be coming. The atmosphere will not lighten. If anything, it gets more oppressive, with such a hollow, hushed sound to it,' the Professor said. 'It's like being buried alive in the Teldorra Catacombs. But thankfully, we have the machine ready. That matters more than us.' Everybody valiantly agreed with that.

'It's still nice, though, to have shelter close,' an apprentice piped up with. 'And – remote control!' There was more agreement, and some strungified chuckles.

But Sanskril dallied around his ingenious invention when the others had gone, except for Edrak. The youth had let the last lift-load grindingly go without him, and had loyally returned to his mentor.

'There are no niggling doubts wriggling in, Edrak. I think I cannot drag myself from my life's work.' Sanskril smiled, his pebble-sharp, shiny, own worshipper's eyes staying a fixture on the 'metal deity'.

'You must, Sir,' the sobering Edrak replied. 'As you say,

another storm is in the air. Unless the one before has never really left it.'

'A good point, my boy! And studying this divergence too from the normal will be on the list for that next pressing issue. Meanwhile, I have to admit I do have a hankering to manually activate the machine at the first lightning prong sear. It would be of more effect! But worry not! I can withstand the hankering. I wouldn't care to be the stereotype mad scientist hand-on-lever before the Zalan bolt!'

Edrak was relieved about that.

And he ought to have enjoyed the full cup of it.

He wasn't to be relieved about anything again.

At the Moon Star, the panic was rising once more. Terror and turmoil, back in wilder waves through the bulging Tavern. With one affrighted voice speaking for all, against the grating clang of the re-closing shutters, 'Another storm. It has to be – you need a rock-cutter on the atmosphere!'

Which were nearly the same words from the troubled enough Hahn, of the westerly searchers for Soletra. This the new signpost reading pell mell for them to their nearest shelter – with poor Rhada having to be heaved along there, when he would have teetered blindly and berserkly onwards to the blue fern gully.

Those far-off at the Vaal Institute, monitoring Sanskril's progress, were also beginning to suspect… The interference on visual, and the audio static, on their way to suppressing all transmissions.

As for Krael, he was hardly out of one tranquil sector into the untranquil other, when his small, slimline ship bumped onto the path of turbulence, and thunder on its fresh warning schedule rumbled over the choppier whine of the vessel.

'Oh no,' he gulped, letting the vessel lurch a lot more, and having to reduce his speed, as advisable for shoddy piloting.

'Oh no!'

And on Dallan-Torrin… Edrak's remarks on more of the out-of-the-ordinary thunder, and with its no lightning yet, trailed off when he spotted the small air shuttle appear in the dark, thundery distance beyond the dimmed floods. Sanskril, with whom the youth had been about to take the lift now only biding for them, saw the vessel from him.

'But there should be no unauthorised craft over this area tonight,' the Professor said, with Arca owl blinks behind his spectacles. 'What kind of craft is it? And why is it here?'

'It's not flying well.' Edrak was firstly concerned with the erratic tipping and dipping of the nose lights, not just for a defective atmosphere. He was more concerned when the vessel got nearer and wrenched itself from the dark into the fawn-ish floods, and into the better scope of his eyes on the whetstone. 'It's one of ours, Sir!' he exclaimed. 'One of the racers.'

'I requested no vessels from Vaal before our faulty and failing communications between us and the Institute! And none would fly here unrequested!' Sanskril said, with a flurry of blinking from eyes too weakened by study to distinguish over any distance. 'Could your transmitter make ship's contact at this radius?'

Edrak tried, to unsociably louder static. 'Sorry, Sir. It can't be done, even at this short radius, and with my transmitter more than suitable for the task. All communication is out for the brewing weather. And we should be leaving; the others will be almost at the train. But the racer is surely heading for the plateau in its reckless veerings, and whoever is in it could be needing assistance!'

'You will all of you be needing assistance. Never fear!' the voice said from somewhere at the back of them, when everybody else had gone and there should be nobody there. A voice that razored the laden air apart, and made flesh cringe and hair stand on end. That was heatedly lively with its keenness, yet had a reptilian slide to it, and dripped through the subtle strainer of mockery and scorn, a deadly, caustic venom of hate and malevolence.

Edrak and the Professor wheeled round, with colliding gasps and hearts instantly braking to the same overturning halt, at the dread sound of that voice, more than the downright surprise of it.

And if each of them had thought they knew what shock, fear, and horror was – the elder from a lifetime of experiences on this and many worlds; the younger from his only real experiences on the one world in just this one night, amounting to a teaching life time for him – they could never have been more mistaken.

Here and now was the truest meaning of these worst emotions to be found. It even nullified incredibility.

The mouth of hell could have all at once yawned open at their feet (and might well have, to explain an appearance from nowhere) and unleashed what they were seeing from its heathenish, heinous lowest depths.

Scientist and student were as if changed to stone, that might soon shatter into a million mortified pieces.

Krael wanted to land nearer to the machine, like that Taraid metal invader on its cliff top, and the two figures getting plainer in its rigid, queer pattern of shade. But he could be having to land quicker. He wasn't an A1 pilot, to begin with, and adding to that the turbulence in the air, and in him from fear now given a name, he was bodging it, losing flight integrity.

He did land quicker. But not only for that. It was what he saw next on that headland of Dallan-Torrin, which could have changed him to stone, too.

…The horrid materialisation. A conjuring as if by the blackest magic. With its own lurid lights in the dimmer floods.

All that should never be. Yet was.

Although he hadn't been unprepared – armed with the knowledge from an ancient script, a name in Yalskrid had certainly presented the key to – he still hadn't been prepared for this.

Krael landed deplorably, but safely enough. He was just an offence to the rule book. A side-tilting settle was frowned upon. He was out of the little ship in a jellified jiffy, gulping breaths of the damp, lead air going to cold condensation inside him, and collecting himself, hit and miss, for his foisted-upon destiny.

Edrak dumbfoundedly recognised him. From that description furnished with unnerve and unease.

…The handsome, animated, cruel, sardonic face, with the bedazing, brain and spirit-soldering, red fire eyes reflecting frightfully on it. The long hair, as red a riotous rippling like it could ignite the atmosphere and the cut floods. The tall, guile-fully graceful figure swept in the reams of blackest cloak, with the eerily 3D, ugly slime shines to it, and the rustle more of wicked, scheming whispers.

The magnificence and the malignance of the Star Wanderer.

The evil in full exposure.

But the youth barely recognised, his fragmented mind grappling for a grasp on it, she who was standing beside the baleful being. With her same long hair flowing into his, lime green curlings surging amidst those of the pigment of living flame. The cool, with the hot.

It was Soletra. Yet it wasn't.

The girl's green glory of hair was the only colour left in her. The rest of her – her face and eyes, her form, and a gown the texture of vapour it was inadequately dressed in – was all cast in a pale, translucent glow, making more of a spectre of her than somebody alive. That face also was lovely no more in its dear way of sweetness and innocence. It had a cold, hard, impassive beauty, with her eyes that emerged frosted in their pallor, like the glaciers of the ice sector on the northern continent. And her body, that had always been shapely but virtuous with her shyness and modesty, now seductively flaunted itself, be it in that carried on coldness and impassiveness. Its extra luscious lines and curves shamelessly paraded through the diaphanous robe, with its vapours like ever mists from those ice lands, which furled and unfurled slowly and ethereally to no movement. Soletra stood still as a statue and sighed, as did the freezing winds on the icicled heights, to the profane whisperings of the cloak.

'Soletra! No – no! It… it can't be!' Somehow Edrak

expelled that past the crushing, stony fingers on his throat. But could that have been his own voice?

Sanskril, who had never been utterly bereft of speech in all his fifty odd years, was then, and some over. He could only stare from behind spectacle glass that could have cracked at that most terrible of sights!

The awful pair, however they had got there – without the lift, or a shuttle – and without being seen, heard or sensed, as well. The fiend of a man with his leering, volatile, virulent evil, who burned like a fire. And the cold, emotionless ghost of a girl, like a pale smoke of the fire.

'Soletra! No! No!' Edrak numbly reiterated it, now in a more bewilderedly horrified groan that could have been in the prezla nut grinder.

The girl looked back at him, and seemingly right through him. As if she didn't know him, either – as if she never had! Then she spoke. Similarly, it was Soletra's voice. And it wasn't. It was as cold, hard, and expressionless as her face, as she said to the youth, her betrothed: 'Run. Run. While you can.'

Edrak was fast mute again. And under both the callous iced gaze and the gloating fiery one, he could have been brought to his shaken knees. But Professor Sanskril battled out of his dumbstruckness at the glacial words of threat. He hackedly and hoarsely addressed the real and the unreal personages imbuing the night and the place with their awfulness transcending that of the hovering storm.

'Who, in all the universe, are you?' he entreated, especially unable to believe, in his own horror, that the pallid, unfeeling wraith creature could be the dear Soletra Edrak had incessantly extolled to the skies for the chaste, caring, gentle wonder of her. 'How… did you get up here? Without any visible means? Without us seeing? Why… are you here?'

It was the wraith that answered him.

'Run, too, little man. Clever little man.' With the threat in the chill, and the unearthliness, for him also.

And if the scientist's blood hadn't already been injected with the ice of her, that would have secured it, and the frozen sparking of her hueless eyes.

'No. The chance to flee is not his,' her dread companion said, ending his mocking verbal abstinence. That conversely heated blade of his tongue slashing into the vaporous, iceberg imperviousness. 'Not that clever, strutting little man indeed!'

And to that last sentence, and the extremity of vindictiveness and despise, a dark arm rose, raining slippery folds of whispery cloak. But not to inflict a blow, only hurl an invisible force which threw Sanskril, who couldn't move of his own volition, feet into the air and twistedly backwards onto the ground. The Professor fell very heavily, his head just missing one of the tripod's metal legs, smashing the remote control disc that he'd had magnetised to his belt. He lay there. Incapable of getting up. He felt as if every joint in his body had disjointed. He could do no more than moan with pain.

The terrible stranger laughed low and pleasurably, his arm still dramatically raised in glideful falls of cloak.

This act of violence propelled Edrak out of his own immobility in a different way. His anxiety for his mentor bursting forth in the size of more horror, tore him from the black witchery of his apparition sweetheart and the demon incarnate, and took him half tumbling to Sanskril's recumbent side.

'I have not finished with him yet. Though he may wish I

had!' was sneered after Edrak, on the edges of the villainous laughter. While in more direly startling conjunction with that, and as Edrak was fully focussing on the suffering Sanskril, the stranger – whoever, he could be to have such power – began to emit a glow himself, but of the brighter kind. Nothing like the ghostly wanness of the girl – whoever, whatever, she was now, too.

The glow swiftly suffused all of him, his darkly beautiful face and ocean-waving hair, his snakishly sensational figure and the repellent cloak about that aplenty, and it got brighter and brighter by the alarmingly astounding second, stamping him dismayingly more, as was never needed, out of the floods made even dimmer to that.

It got brighter and brighter. Brighter. And brighter. And brighter. Until, the only colour somehow remaining in the fellow was that of his eyes – two crimson, jungle cat slants. Everywhere else he just radiated a white-hot light, more like a terrific, pure cosmic energy than anything fire-related that could blisteringly blind and burn as much.

White heat… with slits of red heat that were that devil looking as ever potently through.

He could never be more dreadful. Could he?

And Soletra there beside him – the Soletra, and not her –seemed to be starting to intermerge with him. Slowly and spectrally. Horribly and inexplicably. Her pale, misty translu-cence bathed in his greater brightness, a mirror of shimmerous haze for it, melting into that brightness… and next seeming to increase it. Making the less of her – for the more of him.

Sanskril, seeing past Edrak what was happening here, partly forgot his pain, his moans ragging off into a single, rawly suspended gasp for the outer limits of the unimaginable attained. Edrak, on his bended knee, turned back at that, to also see… what it was, and could never be.

The man in hot white dazzle, including the cloak then hissing where it had whispered, but for the hot red dazzle of the eyes poisonously the expression centre of the face in the ray. The girl fading into him, dissolving into him, pale particles of vapour vanishing as pinpricks of flash into the ignitable white brilliance, being consumed by him, and aiding what unholy transformation he was undergoing. And all of it with her cold, emotionless willingness, to his malicious joy and triumph.

'Soletra! Soletra! No!' Edrak shouted to her he saw most. Shouted in the horror and terror that couldn't possibly get any worse. And yet did! 'No!'

The man-monster, in his sheeting, eating white, stared excruciatingly at Edrak through it, and leered at him. 'You can save her no more than you can save yourselves! Not that she would want you to!'

'No! NO!' But Edrak went on torturedly shouting it. For Soletra – the Soletra that used to be, and just had to be there still, who was diminishing before him with rightly enough coldly consenting ease.

'By all the blessed and the divine that this is not! What is to be!' Sanskril frayedly rasped, more from appalled spirit than broken body, on Edrak's agonised echoes. 'What is to be!' With his repetition in further gripes swallowed off, as he was dazedly aware of a third person entering the hellish tableau imprinted on those more reduced floodlights.

He blearily distinguished the luckless newcomer as a youth of Edrak's age, slim in the tousled Vaal tunic, and with tan hair spraying loose from its semi braids. The hair swung like a curtain to his lurching run, where his legs could have been forging through the Wastran waters against its exacting current, because of the urgency and fear too much for them. The Professor found his face familiar, but no name to go with it.

Krael shook to outdo the judder leaf, but he stood his canting ground with the valour he'd never thought was his.

The terribly-changing stranger had let him get near. The red burning brand for his stare told the fresh player on the dark scene that his knowledge was no secret from him, and only worthy of his sneering contempt, like the bravery with the knowledge. He said to Krael – his voice a scalding, many-tailed whip to scourge the youth's shrinking body, as the eyes were the furnace grids for his shrinking brain, heart, and soul: 'You should not even dare to contemplate it. That what you have learned in the providential fashion you have, could be to your, or anybody's avail in the false face of me, never mind the true!'

Krael had no reply to this. However, the evil entity did know the lad knew. Whether it was from the 'all discerning' gaze of mocking malignance, or the felt ghastly presence in a creepy cellar – as he could do almost anything already.

'Nothing can stop me now. With the chosen who is able to look upon me – at last. And want to be, and yet be not.' The voice continued flailingly, with more venom dripping from the lash tails. 'This night will I shed the skin of Jadaras forever, and become that destroyer indestructible. The power absolute to end the age and the dominion of all mortal life, especially man.

'This world shall fall before me, and every other world and galaxy then open up to me… until the universe is mine. And with it, the gateway of its sentinels also slain, to the mutated universe behind, in the 7th dimension of shadow, the accursed Nethren–Kha, from which the guardian of all evils, and his legions, will be summoned forth. No. Nothing can stop me! And you, foolhardy young meddler and confronter, you shall only die harder yourself for both!'

But hanging by his gritted teeth onto the one sole hope he'd got to envisaging, Krael prised his terrifiedly fascinated attention from the undreamed-of adversary, with imprecations fitting his foul lips, before it could be fatal to him right there, and switched it in dithers of duress to his friend, who was as oblivious of him as he could be. Edrak, cockling against the tripod, and dumbly pouring all his emotions to scrape the grievous barrel of them into the splitting mould of panic at his Soletra going faster into the radiance of the damned.

'Edrak! EDRAK! Hear me! Do what you are here for!' Krael called to him, his desperate timbres axing into the stone wall solidity of the air that could have dashed them back. But there was no response. Edrak didn't hear him, any more than he saw him.

'EDRAK!' Krael upped the scale to a yell on barbs. It only glanced off deaf ears again.

Sanskril, past surprise and ponder for why Krael was actually here, writhingly supplicated him, 'What are you on about, boy?'

'He must just listen to me!' Krael frenetically replied to him.

'And what good will that do?'

'Give us the only hope we have! Trust me, Professor, Sir! Please!'

The Professor did. There wasn't anything else to do. He wrackedly called himself to Edrak. And this time Edrak heard, as it was more from the trained reflex of the student hearing the master, the tormented blond and copper head listing in a return to the scientist.

Sanskril at once painedly put the order to the call, stating in it, 'And it – has to – be the lever – the remote is – as useless – as me…' With Krael bethinkingly endorsing all that in more of the verbal shakes. 'It's only how you can help Soletra!'

'Fools indeed!' The stranger – the he or the it – just jeeringly laughed at Krael and Sanskril, as his burn-white rays dwindled still faster the paler, fainter glimmers of a girl, those that comprised his hissing cloak starting to drip, like the poison in his eyes and on his tongue. Sparking white drops that became bigger, and more like torn clumps of white flame fabric, which stayed blazingly so on the ground, as the earlier mere drips corroded the bare rock. Krael alone noticed the 'sheddings' that, what he didn't know, had begun in advance. In the colour of black on Tarra Myya. And he was about to panic, too, another yell on fright thorns to its gathering surge, 'Hurry, Edrak! For pity's sake! Hurry!'

He – it – laughed derisively louder at Krael. He laughed at Sanskril in his agonies that had contorted his perplexedly frantic order along with his crooked body. He laughed at Edrak as the half-crazed lad then reacted to that order from Krael's penetrating endorsement and enforcement. He laughed as the Valadrian's lever cranked jaggily down under a numb, shivering hand, and the machine was all lit and humming, as it had been shortly ago in savoured jubilation seeming gone to the Draaga dogs. Was all alive with its own electrical brilliance, majesty and might, its own fearful import and portent. Edrak and Krael on the splintered rebound; Krael from his first experience of the machine launching into life, and Edrak from what he had actually done.

The fiend laughed and laughed. That sound as awful, malevolent, and deadly as the rest of him.

He laughed and laughed. In his unconquerable supremacy. And his heights of disdainful relish for this capping folly and futility of morons and their fancy, bright new toy!

Laughed and laughed. With the neglected, still wrongly lightningless thunder rolling more noisily close, to now be as relishingly an accompanist, and to as exultantly augment the next stupefying phase of the monster's transmutation, this taking him to where the hot whiteness of him was unexpectedly digressing, steaming into tints of the holding hue of his eyes.

Edrak, giddily pivoting round to reclaim his stressed sight of Soletra, saw what was coming then through the sharp sparkles of bluey-green and amber added to the general dazzle. And he did go weakly back onto his knees. Professor Sanskril, seeing the same in strobe lights, couldn't sink any lower than he was, but he forgot his pain altogether, and maybe for ever more. Krael just stood there. In knowing. And waiting. And the waxing only one glaring colour for him.

The thunder rolled and rolled until it was right overhead in worsening, visible clashes of cloud, a sky sea getting to the boil. Then it cracked into an instantaneous ear-splitting peal, as if fully proclaiming its triumph and extolling for the one, and his final crossing of the threshold. The peal lasted for deafening ages, and was only fast and surpassingly repeated on the crashing crux, where it was like to stone deafen, bring down that agitating sky, and make the plateau quake enough to sprout fissures wide and deep, for things to tumble into, such as students, scientists, and machines.

There was no just 'as if it was' about it. The thunder was rejoicing… it was lauding… and exhorting on…. and, along with that, it was preparing for something else…. at it being crossed. Whatever that devilish divide…

Edrak and Sanskril felt they were only a seized-up heart and pulse throb from madness.

And Krael felt his teeth grip giving…

But, all of a sudden, when the raggedy hope was nearly no more, and a down coming sky or an opening Torrin crevice seemed a far better mercy, there was another transformation in that personifier of utter evil from whence he was! A more rapid transformation, where his blinding light of new dreader hues was being usurped upon, and warred against by a second, just as blinding light of bluey-green, with amber sparkings, that had a look of gaining ascendance.

There was also a rapid, and still more unbelievable, change in the vile attitude of the fiend further enveloped in the battle glows.

With as sudden a roaring cry of wild, baffled incredulity himself, he ferociously flamed out of his malicious jubilation and gloating, and his contempt stinging tonight like hordes of Zed bees, and was a thwartedly livid, ranting, and raging thing. It made him even more petrifying to behold, and might even have got the accomplice thunder to cower, did it not seem to be immediately retreating, its peals ringing down to protesting rumbles, from the fulgent fight.

'No! No! It cannot be! It cannot!' At the progressingly plainer blue and amber victor, the roar sharded into a shriller cry of the incredulity and the helpless fury. 'This, from the puny intelligence of man, can never be! I am not to be flouted and routed by life so low it has scarcely crawled from the swamps! It cannot be! Never! NEVER!' Which was soon followed by his other cry, with the screeching words in that severing off into a demented incoherence, when the almost taken Soletra wraith was by some way ripped arduously out of him, and away from him, and flung onto the ground as the living Soletra in tendrils of her evaporating translucence, and sheeny remains of his light of colour conflict; whether or not the girl would survive long, or ever be the same again if she was to…

He reached for her with a grasping hand of that coloured fire. But she was beyond its sizzling scope, in her solidified sprawl of showers of hair and drifts of robe. Splashes of the fire hissed on empty rock.

He howled with every ounce of his baulked wrath and mindless hate, and stretched exertively farther forwards on the impetus of both. And he howled terribly more, up to the sawing start of a scream, with that other lancing in, as he was pulled back by the winning light, and into it. Deep, and deeper into it, with no amount of Sanskril-type writhings and contortions that could let him re-emerge, and the sheddings of cloak those burning tatters on the ground he'd stood on, smokily disintegrating into the scorching stone at the rate of his engulfment.

Then you couldn't tell between the screams.

And all that was left on Dallan-Torrin were four people and a machine. The Valadrian with its now louder, churning hum, and crackling live cable, and its flashing, sparking colours alone.

'What have I just seen! What have I just seen!' the greatest scientist in the land half babbled, as Edrak could do no more than blankly scrabble on his hands and knees to the unstirring Soletra.

Krael answered Sanskril with a calmness that should never have been his. But was.

'The destroyer… destroyed. Our planet saved, and its time-old curse ended. And maybe the universe saved, too. There is only the dream that cannot be fully ours. As it was ever the matter of the one, not the many. The reborn, not the new.'

'I don't understand.' The genius next humbled himself before the fledgeling academic. 'Who? What was it I could have seen! *We* could have seen! Somebody – something from the terrible, dark places that aren't of legend and fable after all? A super inhuman being with as terrible, dark powers enough to take control of our weather, become even a part of it, for admittedly its master weapon potential?'

'No, Professor,' said Krael the quieter. 'He wasn't from any other world, out of the dark side of myth, or not. He was from here. He was of here. He has always been of here. And as for taking control of our weather, up to becoming a part of it? He never had to do that. In, it has to be, his somehow evilly-endowed state during our evolution, where later his body was separate from his slaying soul, he was our weather.

'Zaltar Valada, do you know what his name is in ancient Yalsrit?'

'Yes. Save us! The Zalan bolt.'

SOLAR EPILOGUE

Many licks of flame sprang from the great machine; all but one extinguishing on the air and the rising wind. The exception, unfathomably igniting itself bigger and brighter, soared upwards and skywards, eventually vanishing through singed swirls of cloud.

It continued far, far on. To leave the very planet, with the surrounding fiery belt making it burn bigger and brighter still, and venture into the endless starry dark of space.

A cryptic cosmic flame, that sometimes rode on the back of an asteroid or the tail of a comet.

Could it be anything other than it was?

Only the universe, in all its majesty, mystery, and wonders, amazing and terrifying, can tell…